Don't Get Caught

JAYE PRATT

Copyright © 2024 by Jaye Pratt, in Australia.

All rights reserved. No part of this publication may be reproduced, stored or transmitted in any form or by any means, electronic, mechanical, photocopying, recording, scanning, or otherwise, without written permission from the publisher. It is illegal to copy this book, post it on a website, or distribute it by any other means without permission.

This novel is entirely a work of fiction. The names, characters, and incidents portrayed in it are the work of the author's imagination. Any resemblance to actual persons, living or dead, events or localities, is entirely coincidental.

Jaye Pratt asserts the moral right to be identified as the author of this work.

Designations used by companies to distinguish their products are often claimed as trademarks. All brand names and product names used in this book and on its cover are trade names, service marks, trademarks, and registered trademarks of their respective owners. The publishers and the book are not associated with any product or vendor mentioned in this book. None of the companies referenced within the book have endorsed the book.

Formatting by Formatting and Design by Jaye.

Editing by Cat Jay PA - Messenger's Memos

Proofread by Kelly Messenger - Messenger's Memos

Blurb

Sometimes life throws you a curve ball. They suck in the moment, but in the long run, you end up being chased by three masked men through a cemetery. Now *that's* the curve ball you want.

My boyfriend was perfect, up until he wasn't. When Mr. Vanilla found out about my deepest, darkest fantasies, he spread them all over campus and shamed me in the worst way possible. I dropped out of college and moved to a small town, where I have just inherited a house from my long-lost grandmother.

I'm determined to get my life back on track and leave my old life behind. Never in my wildest dreams did I expect to be chased by a masked man through a haunted house on my first night in town. Or that he would make good on his promise to bring a friend next time, and then two would turn into three.

I have everything I ever dreamed about with these three masked men. Somehow, they found me exactly when I needed them. Now nothing will get in their way because they want to keep me as theirs.

READ ME

Mum me says,

Please don't have sex with strangers in a cemetery, no matter how good it sounds. You could get thrush, catch STIs, or be unalived. Real-life problems suck, I know, but let's keep this scenario for books where you can read about it from the comfort of your own bed with a man who knows exactly where your clitoris is.

Author me says,

Let that masked man catch you and f*ck you hard against a tree while the dead watch on. You do you, boo. Just make sure he brings his friends for round two and three, and they tag team you in the dark while you have orgasm after orgasm, screaming for them to f*ck you harder.

Things in this book that could be concerning:

-Sexy time with strangers
-Unprotected sexy time (she is on birth control)
-Sexy time in places with dirt
-CNC
-Controlling behavior between the men

This book is **MMMF**, and there are preexisting MM relationships. Harlen and Eli; Harlen and North; Harlen, Eli, and North. Lily fits nicely into their relationship and she might be exactly what they've been looking for to complete their dynamic.

There are lots of sexy scenes between Lily and the men, and a sprinkle of scenes from their preexisting relationships. This short novella is just one big fuck fest, and it's best to read it for yourself.

Chapter One

Lily

The sun dips below the horizon as I pull into the quaint little town of Maple Hollow. And before my grandmother passed, it was the place she called home. The large "Welcome to Maple Hollow" sign is hard to miss as I turn into the gas station, where an elderly man in denim overalls rushes outside as I pull up to the pump.

"Filling up today?" he asks as I exit my beat-up old Honda.

"Please," I reply, and he nods.

I leave the man to it, though it feels odd to let him fill up my car, and I head inside where a younger guy—around my age—stands behind the counter. His eyes follow me as I head toward the back to get a bottle of water. Hopefully, there is a grocery store close by for supplies, as I can't imagine any food being in my newly inherited house.

As I approach to the counter, the man smiles widely.

"Haven't seen you around here before," he says, leaning against the counter.

"That's because I've never been here before. I'm just moving to town today."

He nods, and I suppress a shiver. With his amber-colored gaze and a face made up of all the right angles, the guy is extremely attractive. I love the small-town vibe he is throwing out, but the last thing I need right now is a man to complicate things.

My ex broke up with me three weeks ago. Apparently, he read my diary and then demanded I tell him my deepest, darkest fantasy. It scared him enough he ran for the hills. Charles Williamson Jr. was as vanilla as they come. We met on my first day of college, and when he asked me to be his girlfriend after three weeks of dating, of course I said yes. He courted me, took me on dates, and treated me how a lady should be treated. It was all going well for the first year up until I opened my mouth and told him I'd read about CNC—consensual non-consent. The deeper I read, the further down that rabbit hole I fell. There is absolutely nothing wrong with vanilla sex if it's your preference; however, for me, it wasn't enough. Chase me around the house, pull my hair, and give me something to get my blood pumping. This girl wants a damn orgasm that isn't granted by her own hand.

"What brings a pretty girl like yourself to Maple Hollow? There isn't exactly much here. People who arrive are normally running from something."

"I inherited a house from my grandmother. I honestly thought she died when I was a child."

"You're not Mavis Huckley's granddaughter, are you?"

"I am, indeed. Though I wish I'd had the chance to know her."

The man smiles sweetly. "Just ask around—everyone will have a story about her. I'm Harlen."

"Lily. Nice to meet you," I say, handing him my card to pay.

Along with the house, I was left with a nice sum of money. It's not enough to retire, move to the Maldives, and live out my fantasies—I would need a sugar daddy for that—but it's enough to last me at least a year, maybe longer if I budget. Dropping out of college wasn't the wisest idea, but I couldn't stay. Not when my ex's father is the dean and Charles is the college golden boy. Who, of course, took it upon himself to tell everyone I'm a freak.

Harlen hands me back my card. "The Halloween decorations went up today in the town square. If Miss Easton tries to corner you and ask you to be in the parade, run as fast as you can or tell her you have stage fright. She can be quite convincing. The carnival is set up as well. Maybe I will see you there, and you can save a hayride for me."

"Yeah, maybe," I say as the old man walks back inside.

"I filled up your windshield wiper fluid—it was empty—and you need an oil change. If you're staying around a while, bring her back here and I can do it for you."

"Billy is the only mechanic in town," Harlen adds.

"Boy, what have I told you about serving customers? You don't even work here."

"Well, maybe if you hired someone, I wouldn't have to serve myself and the beautiful lady."

They bicker between themselves while I swipe a town map. I wave as I head outside to my car and slide back into the driver's seat. My GPS says I should only be six minutes from the house.

Pulling out onto the main road, I follow the GPS until it tells me my destination is now on my left, and I let out a sigh as I take in the old, run-down house. It looks nothing like the photo that was emailed to me; clearly the image was not a current one. Stepping out of the car, I inhale deeply, and the scent of dried leaves and smoke fills my nose—a vast difference to the smells of the city.

The house sits between two large trees. The leaves' fall hues mixed with the smell of smoke remind me of the one childhood memory I have of this place, though it's barely even a memory. It was the one and only time my father brought me here. I figured we never came back because she had died—my father even said as much one of the last times I saw him before he left my mom. I have yet to tell her I have dropped out of school and moved ten hours away, not that she would care. She is off traveling the world with her husband, who is a writer of some popular fantasy books. They're not my thing, but millions of people read them. Mom said they are making them into movies, which is cool, and I might watch them then. I don't hate to read, and a good dark romance gets my blood pumping, but fantasy has so much world building my head can't retain all the information.

I look at the house. The paint is peeling on the siding, one of the front windows is cracked, and the garden is overgrown. A gust of wind rustles through the trees, sending a shiver down my spine, but there is something comforting about the chill in the air. This time of the year is my favorite.

The house might not look like much, but it's mine—and with a little TLC, it will soon be back in shape.

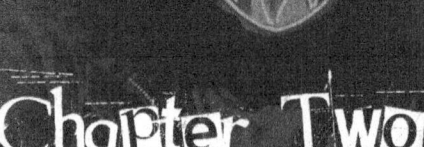

Chapter Two

Lily

Harlen wasn't wrong when he said Halloween decorations were going up in the town square. Even the houses on my short walk are decorated, and I wonder if there is a store that sells them. I feel left out.

As I wander down the main street, children dressed in costumes run around looking at all the decorations. The main street has every shop in the town: a diner, a grocery store, a Christmas shop, a bakery, an ice cream parlor, a post office, a thrift store, and a library right at the end.

A newspaper catches my eye in a street rack outside one of the shops, so I grab a copy off the top of the pile. In large print it says: *The Rumor Report,* and below is a picture of me with a short write-up. I have only been here for two hours, but everyone already knows about my arrival. How did they know I was coming? It must be the estate lawyer.

"I wouldn't take any notice. Small towns and gossip—if you fart wrong, they will write about it. So I suggest you avoid the onion soup at Main Street diner, as I hear it can make you toot."

"Thanks for the warning. I'm not sure why they think I'm running from a dark past. I wish I was that interesting. Though I dropped out of college, so that part's true."

The handsome stranger laughs. His dirty-blonde hair looks like he just rolled out of bed, and his piercing blue eyes crinkle at the corners. "I'm North, and I'm guessing you're Lily, Mavis's long-lost granddaughter."

"That's me," I say, taking his outstretched hand.

"I recommend the haunted trail. It's fun." He points toward the library, where there is a large sign which reads, "Haunted Trail." "The entire side road closes all the way to the cemetery, and they even have the old hospital set up as a haunted house."

"They close an entire road?"

"That road is basically deserted. It only leads to the old hospital, which hasn't been used to treat patients in over a decade. Doctor Stephans has a new building behind the library and any medical emergencies are sent to Willow Grove, the closest town to here. You would have driven through it to get to Maple Hollow—we are the end of the road as far as they are concerned."

"It was nice to meet you, North. I might go check out the haunted house."

"See you around, trouble," he says with a wink, and walks away with his hands shoved in his pockets.

The echo of children's laughter gets louder the closer

I walk to the haunted trail. Halloween is still weeks away, and yet everyone here is committed to capturing the spirit early. Normally we would have only just pulled our decorations out; Mom isn't one to get into the holidays unless it's Christmas. She once left our tree up for an entire year, but looking back, it could have been because my father had only just left and the joy that Christmas brings was exactly what our family needed. A family went from three down to two—or five, if you counted my mother's parents and my uncle Jasper. Three other people I'd yet to tell I left college to move to a small town.

"You must be Lily," an older man says, looking down at the newspaper tightly rolled in my hand.

"That's me," I reply politely. I have a feeling this is going to happen a lot over the coming days.

"I couldn't help but notice you were talking to North. Be mindful of the boy. He and his friends are a rowdy bunch."

"Thanks for the tip. I was hoping to do the haunted trail—Halloween is one of my favorite times of year." What I don't tell the old man is it's because I just finished reading a dark romance focused around Halloween, where the pumpkins turned into ripped men.

"I'm Theodore, the mayor of Maple Hollow. If you need anything, please let me know."

"I will, thank you," I say, then hurry toward the start of the trail.

A teenage girl dressed as a bloody nurse presses a button and creepy laughter comes from the darkened trail.

"Just follow the lights on the ground. Since you're new, we don't allow you to touch anyone who jumps out at you. The second roped-off area is for the adults. If you pass it, I suggest you don't get caught. They will chase you," the girl explains.

I nod and walk through the smoke-filled archway, taking in the decorations. A fake cemetery is set up and as I walk by, a skeleton rattles and scares the life out of me. Continuing on the path, ghosts—sheets with glow sticks inside hung from trees—and random bursts of smoke have a couple of children squealing and running ahead of me. I reach the end of the first path, and a gust of wind sends a chill down my spine. Caution tape ropes off the next area and a large man stands there in overalls and a Jason mask.

"Enter if you dare," he rasps, holding up the tape.

Ducking down, I maneuver underneath it and continue up the driveway of the old hospital. Garbage bags shaped like dead bodies hang from a large tree standing lonely in front of an old, rickety fence, a graveyard hidden just beyond. The sound of a chainsaw starting behind me causes me to turn, and I am confronted by a man in a coat walking up the path. I jog up the dirt path toward the building.

A bloodcurdling scream jolts my heart, and the rattling of a cage comes from beside me. I look down and see a girl shaking the bars of a small cage. "Help me," she says, reaching out to me.

I laugh at myself and run to the front door. It has wood nailed across it and a sign saying, "Keep Out." I push it open and dash into the small lobby, where there is a glow-in-the-dark skeleton behind a desk, and spiderwebs lining the ceiling. The only other door has "Turn back now" written in glow-in-the-dark paint. I step forward to push it open and find a hallway lined with cloaked figures, and a red carpet leading to a red curtain.

My hands sweat—now *this* is the adrenaline I'm after. I damn-well know one of these cloaked figures is a real person, and the anticipation of them jumping out at me has me feeling giddy. Now, if only Charles had been willing to dress up and chase me around our apartment. It wasn't like I was asking him to actually assault me; it would have been simply make-believe. I even offered a safe word so he would know if he took it too far, but he only scoffed and told me the sex books I read had filled my head with filth. How he wouldn't stand for his future wife doing the devil's work. Charles wasn't even religious, so I'm not sure how he came to that conclusion.

Right on cue, as I inch down the red carpet, one of the figures moves. I squeal loudly, even though I knew it was going to happen.

"Run, before he catches you," the cloaked man whispers, pointing behind me. A figure in a red glow mask steps through the door. "Don't get caught."

The masked man moves forward as I duck behind the curtain. This hallway is empty, except the windows of each door have people behind them and I can feel their gazes on me. I don't have time to stop, the masked figure stepping from behind the curtain, and I run down the hall and follow the sign to the left. A note on the door around the corner reads, "Open me if you dare," and I twist the handle, stepping into what looks like an old surgical room. A crazed doctor turns to me, waving a saw covered in fake blood.

The doctor steps toward me, and I wonder what would happen if I didn't move. I don't get to test the theory as the masked man opens the door. I keep moving forward, dodging the doctor and running into the next room. It's designed like an old jail cell, and zombies reach through the bars, the room echoing with their groans. Nope, that's a *fuck no*. Zombies freak me the hell out, even though I know they are not real.

I'm not watching where I'm going as I run through the next door, causing me to trip over my own feet and face-plant. As I push onto my knees, I feel a hand wrap around my ponytail. Hold on, I thought they could not touch you? The pressure of the man pulling me by my hair draws me to a stand, and his front presses against my back.

Wetness pools between my legs. Maybe Charles was right, maybe I *am* sick.

Who gets off on this shit? Me, apparently. For a brief second, I wonder what this man would do if I said he could fuck me if he could catch me.

"Pretty girls like you should not be in a place like this." His voice is deep and husky. What I wouldn't give for him to force me to my knees and tell me I'm a good girl.

"Pretty girls have fantasies about this shit," I mumble under my breath, and he lets my hair go.

"Is that right? Well, I'll give you a head start, and I suggest you don't get caught. Because men like me will take what they want."

Turning back, I look at him over my shoulder. Could he be for real or is this all part of the act?

"Three..."

I don't wait for him to count further—there is only one way to find out.

Chapter Three

Eli

Harlen told North and me there's a pretty new girl in town, but I needed to see for myself. He wasn't wrong—she isn't just pretty, though. She is beautiful.

This is the closest I come to being near people; I rarely leave the house. But this place—the old hospital—we bought a few years back and have been renovating it. North wants it to be a bed-and-breakfast, but Harlen wants it to be a rave spot. A place to host parties where people can travel to and stay. They bicker about it daily, but if they put their heads together, they could do both. I won't voice my opinion—I rarely do, since the accident years ago where my throat was torn open and left my vocal cords damaged.

I don't know why I let Lily hear my voice. No one in town has heard me talk since the day I almost died—they all hate us anyway, so what's the point? We have been causing chaos since we were kids. Over on Pine Street, there was a home for boys where we all grew up. It was run by old man Jenkins, and he used to get us out on the farm to work—it's how I had my accident.

Lily is an attractive woman, and we've had no one new arrive in Maple Hollow for a long time. The last one was Sally Rowland's nephew, Waylen, and he isn't my type—too pretty for my liking. I swing both ways, but I like men to look rugged.

I wasn't supposed to chase the pretty girl so far, but I wanted a closer look without scaring her. And every time she looked back at me, I'd swear it was as if her big blue eyes pleaded with me to chase her. I never intended to wrap my fist around her lucious blonde hair or pull her to her feet, but her scent called to me. North has always said a woman's arousal can be smelled, but surely not unless your face is buried between her legs.

Her eyes rounded like saucers when I whispered in her ear, "Pretty girls like you should not be in a place like this."

Her reply shocked me more. Did she have fantasies about this sort of thing? When I started my countdown, she took off running. But a head start won't help her; I know this place like the back of my hand.

Moving across the room, I see her duck through a door, one which leads outside. I can't hold back my smirk. She is headed into the cemetery, and it's my all-time favorite place. My feet hit the ground fast enough to decrease the distance she has created, but she keeps moving and I keep chasing her through the overgrown grass North has been on my ass about mowing. Joke's on him because this is the most fun I've had in a long time.

She drops behind a tree. While I could turn the mask off and sneak up on her, what fun would that be? When I get closer, she tries to move, but I'm almost twice as big as her—Lily is a tiny little thing. I wrap my hand around her silky hair again and pull her back, then push her face-first into the tree. She struggles against my hold, but I spread my hand flat on the back of her skull and move my body so it is tight against hers. I use my other hand to test the waters, running it along her side. She shivers under my touch, and I slide my hand down until it reaches the top of her jeans. Lily bucks back, pushing her ass hard into my cock.

A deep growl rips through my chest. "If you keep doing that, I will fuck you against this tree."

"Oh no, please don't!" Her words say one thing, but her tone hints at another as she pushes back into me again.

I twist the button on her jeans, it pops open, and I release her hair. Sliding her jeans down just enough, I then pull my hard cock from my sweats and rub the tip along her ass. The feel of her soft, velvety skin against me has precum smearing her crack.

She doesn't fight me, and I dip my tip lower, lower . . . there. Her wetness is warm and welcoming. Fuck it. Harlen only said to make sure I know a girl's name before I fuck them, not that they had to know mine.

I thrust forward, and my eyes roll back in my head.

Her tight, wet cunt hugs me like it was made for me. I need more, so I slide back slowly, savoring the feeling.

"Do you hear the sounds your body is making? Doesn't seem like you're all that scared to me."

Wrapping my hand around the front of her neck, I pull her upright while I'm still balls deep inside her pussy. "I want you to scream for me, fight me."

"Fuck you," she seethes, jabbing her elbow back into my abs.

"No, baby, I'm going to fuck *you*," I say as I pull out of her. "I want you to run deeper into the dark, where only the dead can hear you scream." She turns and blinks at me, and I step forward, pulling her jeans up a little. "If you want my cock again, run!"

She takes off through the gravestones. They are all old and falling apart; some have been here for over a hundred years. She's moving with a fair bit of speed, but she is no match for me—besides, she wants to be caught. She darts and weaves, and as she moves around one particularly large headstone, I come around the other side, launching my body toward hers. She falls to the ground and this time she really fights back, kicking and screaming, and I laugh at her feeble attempt to protect herself.

"You will need to do better than that," I taunt, leaning forward and crushing her body face-down beneath mine. I pull the back of her jeans down again before taking my cock out, and I find her cunt so wet for me it's practically gushing.

Thrusting myself deep inside her, I grin behind my

mask as she screams, then she maneuvers her top half enough so she can reach back and scratch at my hands with her nails, digging them in deep. A chuckle vibrates deep in my chest as I rear back to a kneeling position between her legs and move my hand to her upper back, pressing it into the dirt. Sliding my other hand under her hips, I raise her ass high, then bring my palm down hard against her soft skin—once, twice, three times—and the slaps echo in the darkness.

"Oh fuck! Please!" she cries into the dirt.

I slam back into her, and she screams, then she switches to breathy moans that punctuate my harsh thrusts.

"There is no one here to save you. Old man Joe has been dead for sixty years," I rasp out, knowing each of these graves by heart.

The farm backs onto the other side of the graveyard, and I spent my childhood scrubbing these headstones as punishment when I messed up. It became a time of solitude for me.

I pick up my tempo, and her body tenses beneath me, her needy cunt gripping my dick like a vice. Her cry rings out around us as wetness drips down my balls, and her scent alone is enough to make me come, along with the feel of her orgasm. I grab her hips and pull her back into me, my hips moving of their own accord as I ride out my release.

Pulling out, I stand and tuck myself away, knowing that later, when I take my cock in my hand, I will be able to smell her.

"Next time, don't get caught," I growl out, "because two is better than one."

With that, I turn off my mask and walk away. Maple Hollow is as safe as they come, and she will be fine to make her way into town by herself. She clearly doesn't want a gentleman, and even if I was one, I wouldn't walk into that town.

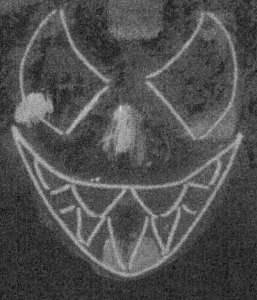

Chapter Four

Lily

I dust myself off, not that it helps remove the grass stains from my clothes. Then I tidy my hair and wipe the tears from my cheeks. They are mostly from happiness, and a little because I just let a stranger fuck me in a cemetery and enjoyed every minute of it. Plus, the fact I orgasmed so hard I felt like my head was going to explode.

As I walk back toward the town square, I hope everyone has gone home and there aren't any witnesses to my walk of shame, as there's no doubt in my mind that I look like a mess.

"Who is out there?" a voice shouts as I near the edge of the graves. "Oh, Lily, it's you."

I pause like a deer in headlights. "Harlen?" I squint a little as the figure gets closer.

"Yeah, it's me, taking a shortcut to get home. Are you okay?"

"Yes, I'm fine. I wandered too far into the cemetery and tripped over. I just need some food and a bath."

"Come on, I will walk you to the diner."

"Oh, you don't have to do that. You're going in the other direction."

He smiles at me. "I'm a gentleman, and you have already fallen over once. It gives me an excuse to say hello to my brother—he owns the diner."

"Okay." I sigh. "I would love the company."

If I'm going to make things work here, I should make friends. But I'm worried he will be able to smell the sex on me and judge me like Charles did. I expect the rumor mill in a small town would be so much worse.

We're walking side by side down the small hill on the other side of the roped-off haunted trail when Harlen breaks the silence. "So, Lily Harper, is everything they say about you in the paper true?"

I glance over at him and he smirks, so I push his arm lightly, making him chuckle. "Only the part about inheriting the house and dropping out of college. Unfortunately, there is no troubled past I'm running from."

"But you were running tonight?" he says with a raised brow.

I don't answer his question, instead countering with my own. "So, what do you do, Harlen, except for not working at the gas station?"

"I like to build things, furniture mainly. There is a shop in the next town over which sells them on commission for me, but I don't really need to work."

"I wish I didn't need to work. What I wouldn't give to

sit by the pool drinking cocktails all day. All I need is a sugar daddy and I'm all set."

Harlen splutters and clears his throat. I clearly took him by surprise with that comment. "Is that what you're into? Old... older men?"

I chuckle at his question. "No, hence why I'm not by a pool right now, sipping cocktails. I guess I will have to find something around here. Know any place hiring?"

"Good luck. Most businesses are family owned, so they hire their children. Other people travel to Willow Grove."

"I have enough money to last me a while, and hopefully the thrift store has a few things I can use for the house. I'll look for a job once I'm settled."

We stop out the front of the diner and Harlen opens the door, the bell chiming as we walk inside. A man who is the spitting image of a slightly older Harlen steps out from the back and frowns at his brother.

"Look what the cat dragged in. Anyone would think you avoid coming here."

"I do because you're a dickhead, but the pretty girl is hungry, and I couldn't let her starve. Lily, meet my older brother, Asher. Not as handsome as me, of course, and he is married," Harlen says. Leaning in a little closer, he adds in a whisper, "His wife is a bitch. She hates me because I live in sin."

"I heard that, Harlen. And she doesn't hate you, she prays for you, there is a difference."

"No amount of prayer will keep things out of my ass.

I keep telling you, a finger in the ass will change your life."

I snort and both men look at me. "What? I can't judge. It would blow your mind if you knew the things I'm into."

Asher runs his gaze over me. "Being tackled into the dirt by the look of you." Then he focuses back on his brother. "And why can't you find a nice girl and settle down? It's time to grow up, have some kids, and stop fucking around with your best friends."

Harlen snorts. "I'm twenty-four, not forty. And there is nothing wrong with fucking my best friends—our situation works for us. Maybe one day we will find a woman, yes, *we*, and then the town will have something else to gossip about."

Asher clears his throat. "Anyway, what can I get you, Lily? I'm sure you don't want to stand there listening to us bicker about his sex life."

"A burger and fries, no tomato, and a water, please."

"Same for me," Harlen says with a smile. "And I'm using your phone."

Asher rolls his eyes at his brother. "Just make it quick. Take a seat, Lily, and I will bring out your food when it's ready."

"Thank you, Asher. It was nice to meet you."

Asher nods and heads behind the counter while I find a seat and pull out my phone. It's almost pointless having it here; there is no reception in this town. I managed to get one bar when I climbed onto the kitchen counter and held the phone on top of the refrigerator to send my best friend, Zoe, a message. All it said was that I arrived safely, and I will get Wi-Fi and a landline installed ASAP.

"So," Harlen says, plopping down into his seat. "What would I be surprised about if I knew?"

My eyes widen as he smiles. "Oh, don't be shy now. I announced how I screw my best friends, and in case you hadn't noticed, this town is very small and not quite caught up with the whole LGBTQIA+ movement yet. Don't get me wrong, most people are polite and only talk about us behind our backs. Mrs. Parkinson likes to play matchmaker and find us each a good girl, but there is no better feeling than asking her to find us one to share."

"I will consider telling you if you answer one question for me."

"What question would that be?"

I inhale deeply, then rush out, "How would sharing one girlfriend work exactly?"

Harlen pushes his dark-brown hair out of his eyes and tucks it behind his ears. "Honestly, we have no idea. We all like women, but life is complicated. Three women under one roof would never work. Eli struggles to talk to us, let alone a woman. North is North—he works hard renovating and flipping houses, but normally crashes by the time he walks in the door. And me, if I'm working on something, I could be locked in the shed for days before I come up for air. One woman wouldn't feel neglected if the three of us shared, but right now, if we have an itch to scratch, we handle it between ourselves."

I nod as he talks. His theory sounds good, but I'm not

sure how it would work in reality. That being said, more power to them for knowing what they want and not conceding to society's pressure.

"I think that's great, knowing what you want and not being afraid to voice it."

Asher interrupts us as he puts our food on the table—the burgers smell amazing—and a woman puts our drinks down.

"Harlen, it's good to see you with a lady friend."

"Agnes, good to see the scowl removed from your face." Asher slaps Harlen on the back of the head, and then they both leave us to eat. "That's his wife. Now finish what you were saying."

His smile is contagious, but I still hesitate a beat. He's the first person I am willingly saying this out loud to. "I like to be scared, chased, forced—or at least I think I do. It's why I'm here, really."

He raises a brow at me. "You came to a small town to be chased and fucked. Hey, no judgment, it's just not where I would have gone looking."

"Says the one who is looking for one woman to share with his friends, who he also shares."

"Touché. Now I want to hear more."

"There isn't much more to tell besides my ex finding out. He told everyone, and it became a thing. He thinks I'm disgusting for even thinking about it."

"His loss," Harlen says, taking a bite of his burger. After he chews and swallows, he adds, "He hit the jackpot and gave it away."

I smile as my chest fills with warmth. He didn't look

at me the way Charles did, so I decide to tell him a little more. "I might have been chased tonight."

His eyes pop up from his plate. "Oh yeah? Anyone I know?"

I shrug. "Not sure who it was. One minute I was in the haunted hospital, and the next thing I knew, I was being chased for real by a man in a glow mask."

His eyes widened. "He didn't . . .?"

"Oh, gosh no. He spoke to me first, kind of, but I gave him consent. I have never felt more alive than I did in those moments. He told me not to get caught again because two is better than one."

"What if it's some old guy with a wrinkly dick?"

I snort at his comment. "He had abs, so it at least narrows it down a little, and honestly, I don't think I care. Not knowing makes it so much better. I don't have to worry and be embarrassed if I see him out in public, and he smelled super nice, like rain on a hot day."

"As long as you weren't hurt and consented. Now let's double back to his warning. Next time he will bring a friend . . . how do you feel about that?"

"Excited. Scared. I have only ever been with Charles, the ex. I was the nerd in high school who never had many friends—we moved around a bit after Dad left. It was hard until I met Zoe in high school, and luckily, mom put down roots and I finished high school in one place. College is when I met Charles, and he was the perfect man on paper: good looks, from a great family, treated me well, and took me on dates. Everything I should have wanted." I cleared my throat and took a sip of water.

"Anyway, enough about me. You said you lived with two friends—I met North earlier; he warned me about the small-town gossip. Who is your other friend?"

"Eli, but you won't see him around. He doesn't really leave the house. He hates people looking at him. He had an accident not long after we first met. We were all sent here for foster care placement as kids. We were made to work, not in an abusive way, but more to keep us busy and out of trouble." Harlen snorts, probably thinking of a childhood memory. "Long story short, North, Eli, and I were inseparable from the day we met. Kids came and went, but not us. Asher was taken in eventually by a nice family—he was a good kid and worked hard. It's how he married Agnes. Her family took him in, and he worked on their land. Eventually he saved enough to buy this place. It used to be a video store, but everyone in town had seen everything so many times and streaming services became popular, so Miss Betty sold it to him for cheap."

We talk while we eat, and before I know it, our food is gone and Harlen is walking me home. It might only be my first night, but I have a feeling I'm going to love it here.

Chapter Five

Harlen

When I arrived home last night after walking Lily home, Eli was nowhere to be found, but it's normal for him to vanish right when you really need to talk to him. North just left for an overnight trip for work and won't be home tonight; they are on a job a couple of hours away, and his crew will work through the night to get the job done quicker.

A door slams, and Eli strides in, covered in paint. Sometimes when he gets stuck in his own head, he will paint for hours. Fuck knows where exactly—when asked he says it's his spot and we can mind our business.

"It's going to rain," he announces when he walks into the kitchen, as if he wasn't gone all night, then opens the fridge. When he closes the door, he turns to look at me, picking up on the fact I'm pissed off. He raises a brow, locking his eyes with mine in a standoff.

I break first, moving in closer to him. Eli watches as I

approach, not saying anything, and when I reach him, I knock the bottle of water from his hands. He smirks at me. He knows I know, and yet he thinks it's funny.

"Were you going to tell us?"

The asshole shrugs and steps forward so we are chest to chest.

"Maybe," he says, taking hold of the top of my sweats.

My cock comes to life, ignoring that fact we are furious with him. Sure, we screw girls—well, North and I do. Eli doesn't trust himself, and yet he was comfortable enough to talk to her and chase her through the cemetery. He takes my length in his large, rough hand and strokes me.

"You should have told me. I would have watched from a distance."

"I was fine, I didn't hurt her. Besides, I told her I would bring a friend next time."

"I know. She spilled it all to me last night at the diner after Asher and I had words in front of her about me liking things in my ass."

Eli snorts. "Agnes again?"

I nod as I moan. Fuck, he knows how to work my cock just the way I like it. He lowers himself to his knees. "I'm sorry I didn't invite you, but it just happened. I made sure she consented—twice."

"Good boy, now spit on my cock and show me how well you take me."

He does as he's told, then uses his hand to spread his saliva down my length before bringing his mouth to my now hard-as-fuck cock. As he wraps his lips around the head, I buck forward, forcing myself down his throat. "I don't like feeling jealous, Eli. You know that. I'm possessive and would have killed to watch you fuck the pretty girl into the dirt. Do you know how hard I was when I realized her story was about you? I'm pissed you trusted her enough to talk to her."

He hums as he cups my balls. As I thrust deeper into his throat, his eyes water. I wonder if she cried for him. "You will always be mine, Eli. Fucking *always*. I don't mind sharing you with North, or a pretty girl," I say, as I spear my fingers into his hair. Gripping a handful of strands just long enough to use as leverage, I rip his head up so he can look at me, my cock slipping from his lips. "I will drag your ass to the town square and the entire town can watch you suck my dick. Do you understand me?"

He nods as I release his hair and wrap my hand around my cock. I pump it in front of his face, and he waits, knowing I am about to claim him as mine. Cum spurts out of me, and everything I have saved for him lands all over his face, lips, and tongue. "Now, go clean up. We have a pretty girl to chase."

He smirks at me as he licks his lips.

Tonight is going to be fun. I hope Lily is ready.

We wait until after ten to leave, our glow masks in hand. If Lily wants to be chased and fucked hard, she stumbled upon the right town. Eli knows the talking is up to him, and if I'm being honest, I'm hard at the thought of hearing him talk to her. We walk side by side across the empty town square, as it normally is at this time on a Sunday night. All the businesses close early, and while the diner and grocery store are open until eight, it's well past that time.

When we get to Lily's house, all the lights are off. Her grandmother used to leave a key under the welcome mat—most people in town do, as no one gets in or out of Maple Hollow without everyone knowing. Crime is zero now that Eli, North, and I have grown, not that we ever did anything too serious. They were pranks really, reserved for when someone made a stupid comment about the way Eli looks, or when they threw out slurs. Tom Morgan was the worst, so North and I fucked every girlfriend he's ever had, including his wife. We haven't made it known about his wife yet, and we've held that nugget of information for the last year, waiting to drop that bomb when the time is right. We must play our cards carefully now since he is a deputy and would find any reason to arrest our asses.

Eli lifts the mat and holds up the key, then slides it silently into the lock and opens the door. As we step inside, we pull our masks down and switch them on. The red lights illuminate the living area, which hasn't changed since we used to help Mavis change her light bulbs. She was one of the few people in this town who truly accepted us.

"I don't give a damn what you do in the privacy of your own home. You boys have grown into men to be proud of."

Sure, Mavis may have been the one who caught us digging up a grave as boys, but we'd only wanted some old bones to scare people. The crazy woman used to visit her late husband at the cemetery after dark, and she wasn't scared of anything. That night she even kept watch, so we didn't get busted. Though the mayor at the time didn't think it was funny when we set up his great-great-great-grandfather's bones under the gazebo in the town square with a cigar glued in his jaw.

I motion for us to climb the stairs and Eli nods. Halfway up, the old stairs creak beneath my boots. We both pause and listen for any movement . . . nothing. So we keep going up. When we reach the top step, Eli points to a room and I step forward to twist the handle. As I push the door open, I duck just in time to avoid a lamp flying at my head. Glancing back when there's no crash, I spot Eli holding it in one of his large hands. Nice save. I step into the room, and Lily now stands on her bed in her pajamas—I almost laugh at the little ducks on the material.

"What do you want?" she asks, but not loud enough to alarm any of the neighboring houses.

"I warned you I would be back," Eli says, as he steps into the room. Her eyes go wide as she glances between us.

"Please don't hurt me," she whimpers, and Eli freezes mid step. I pull the rope from my back pocket and throw it his way, snapping him out of his trance.

"We don't want to hurt you, baby, we just want to use your holes."

Now it's my turn to freeze. *Baby.* Well that's new. He takes another step toward her, and she jumps off the bed, working out if she can run from his advance. Lily pivots around him and runs toward me, but while I might be slimmer than Eli, she is no match for me. Even if I appear the lesser of two evils. What I don't expect is for her to drop at the last minute and grab me by my nuts, then as I collapse to the ground, she jumps up and darts past me. Eli chases her while I lay on the floor, waiting for my poor balls to come back out of hiding.

Furniture smashes downstairs and I'm jealous I'm not witnessing this chase.

"Let me go!" Her words say one thing, but the hint of excitement in her tone tells us a completely different story.

The sound of Eli's footsteps coming back up the stairs has me pushing to a sit, finally able to breathe again. He has her thrown over his shoulder while she beats against his back. As he tosses her down on the bed, he pulls out his switchblade, and her eyes widen in fear. I can't help the smile which blooms beneath my mask.

Eli cuts the long rope in half, and in half again, and right now I'm thankful old Mavis has a four-poster bed frame. I hurry over and pin her down before she makes another break for it while Eli ties her securely. She tries to kick and curse, but once it's done, Eli climbs on top of her with his knife still in hand. As he runs the blade down the side of Lily's face, her fight becomes real, the fear she so desperately wanted clear on her face.

"You know you want this. I bet your pretty cunt is dripping."

Eli shimmies back so he is now kneeling between her spread legs, then he grabs the material of her pajama pants and pulls it away from her body, using the knife to slice through the cartoon ducks like butter. He doesn't bother cutting the legs off, just removes the crotch, and the obstacle of her underwear is gone just as easily. He drops the blade and plunges his fingers between her legs, moving them in and out. She pulls frantically at her arm restraints and tries to sit up, but it's no use. If Eli ties you up, you're stuck like that until he unties you.

"So fucking wet, baby."

He motions with his head for me to move closer. I'm so hard, I need to come so badly. I sit on the edge of the bed, then I place my hand on her thigh and slide it slowly up the inside of her leg. Eli removes his hand, and the tips of my fingers are the first to feel how wet she really is; Lily wasn't kidding when she said this shit got her off. Delving my fingers inside her, I curl them up and find her G-spot easily.

"Oh, fuck!" she screams, this time loud enough the entire street would hear.

I quickly remove my hand before some do-gooder knocks on her door. Reaching over, I take Eli's knife and climb onto the bed, throwing my leg over her torso and straddling her breasts. As I lean forward, I press the blunt side of the blade to her neck; I don't want to chance hurting her. With my other hand I pull my hard cock from my sweats, then grit my teeth through the discomfort as I bend it downward and smear my precum against her lips.

She smashes her lips closed. Oh, now she wants to play hard to get? Well, two can play that game.

"Let him fuck your pretty little mouth. You don't want to get hurt," Eli says in his husky growl.

I drop the blade beside her head and slide my hand behind her neck, forcing her into a better position for my cock to fill her mouth. I want Eli to fuck her. *That* I need to see, and I want to taste her on him later when I suck his cock clean for being a good boy.

Pressing my tip to her mouth, I make a low sound of approval as she reluctantly opens. As my cock slides inside, I rotate my hips, inching further with each thrust, slowly giving her a chance to adjust to my girth. She gags around me as I press forward with a stifled groan. Hmm, so it seems Lily has a gag reflex, and it feels fucking fantastic.

She moans around my cock, and I glance back over my shoulder—fuck me, Eli is full of surprises. He has his mask pulled up and his head buried between her legs. Eli has always been a quick learner—he listens to cues—and simply knowing what he is doing has me pulling my cock from her mouth so I can hear the sounds she is making. Palming myself, I lower her head back down, but keep my body where it is to block her view of Eli.

"Oh, fuck yes!" she cries out. "Don't stop, please don't . . ."

I jerk myself, watching the pleasure play over her face, waiting for her to come. Her body trembles beneath me. She watches my every stroke through lowered lashes, and I bet she wonders who is beneath the mask. This beautiful woman who likes to be fucked by masked strangers. The telltale tingle and the tightening of my balls has me leaning forward, angling myself as I come in spurts against her lips. With the last spasm, I lean back on my haunches, looking down at my masterpiece. Using my thumb, I rub my cum against her pink lips and push it between them. Her mouth opens and her eyes roll back in her head.

"Oh, my fucking god!" she screams as she writhes and bucks her hips.

I look back over my shoulder as Eli wipes his face with his hand and winks at me before pulling his mask down. Lifting my leg over her body, I tuck myself away and move to the edge of the bed. Sitting beside her once again, I slide my fingers into her pussy, scissoring them. She is more than ready to take Eli, but I need my fingers nice and lubed for what I want to do. I pull out and slide them down her crack, but she sucks her ass cheeks together.

"Not in my ass . . . I have never."

"It's too late for demands," Eli growls, moving his pants down his legs until his huge cock flicks up and hits his shirt-covered abs. I continue to rim her ass with my finger while she tenses, but I wait until Eli climbs on top of her before pushing further. He slips one of his hands under the base of her spine to lift her hips, then he slowly pushes inside her.

"It's so big," she whispers, as she arches her back.

With her mind now elsewhere, I push a finger in her ass, and I can feel Eli's cock rubbing against me.

"Oh my, yes, oh god!"

Her cries of pleasure fill the room as I match my pace to Eli's. Finding someone like Lily is like finding a needle in a haystack. This is going to be a wild ride.

Chapter Six

Lily

Who would have thought it was possible to pass out from too many orgasms? Not me. Never in my wildest dreams did I ever think I would enjoy someone fingering my ass, but here I am, squeezing my legs together at the mere thought.

When I woke this morning, I was unrestrained, tucked in, and had the little knife placed on top of my pillow. I smiled at the gift they left me. Two were just as fun, if not more. Will he bring his friend again? How long will he wait? They're questions I can't get the answers to because I don't know who he is.

"Lily," Zoe snaps.

"Shit, sorry," I reply with a grimace. My ability to concentrate is in shambles.

Thankfully, my phone and internet were connected this morning, and the man who installed it said it was a personal favor from the mayor. Although I really don't want to owe anyone anything, living without a cellphone signal sucks.

"He said he misses you."

"Well, he can go find himself a good little wife. I don't want to talk to him."

"I wouldn't either, with all the crazy sex you're having. I hope you are being safe."

I kind of am. I mean, I'm on the pill. Could I catch an STI? Sure, but this is not a situation where I can ask to see a clean bill of health. "Safe enough—I'm not dead yet."

Zoe harrumphs good-naturedly. "You know I'm your biggest supporter, but I just don't want you calling me in tears because you have lumps on your vajayjay. Then I would have to drive all the way out there to vajazzle it."

"I don't know why you want to look at people's bits all day."

She chuckles at that. "The women here pay good money, and it helps pay my way through college. Anyway, girl, I have to get to class and hope I don't run into your ex."

"Go, learn some things so you can be rich and live your best life. Who needs a sugar daddy when your bestie is destined for greatness?"

"Love you," she says.

"Love you too."

As we end the call, I grab my bag. I need to go to the thrift store and see if I can get some replacement dinnerware, since last night I broke most of the plates and a side lamp in the living room. It was one hundred percent worth it, though.

The best thing about Maple Hollow is being able to walk everywhere. I would need to drive to the gas station, and to visit someone who lives further away from the town square—or if I was in a hurry. But today, I feel amazing, and even though the air is cool, the sun is out.

My first stop is the diner, as I still haven't gone grocery shopping, but I only remember that when I reach the diner and curse myself for not driving.

"What's that face for?"

Looking up, I find North smiling at me. His blonde hair is neatly cut, and he looks like he has just stepped off a construction site.

"I should have driven—I forgot I need groceries."

"I can give you a lift, but I was going to have breakfast first."

"Are you sure? I would hate to bother you."

He chuckles. "It's no bother. I'm only heading into Willow Grove to get some things from the hardware store, and your house is on the way."

"Then the least I can do is buy you breakfast." He opens his mouth to argue, but I cut him off. "I won't take no for an answer."

He nods, opening the door to the diner, and I step inside. Asher looks up from the book he is reading and smiles. North walks to the counter and takes a seat, and I sit beside him. Asher places a mug down in front of North and pours him a black coffee from the pot. "Would you like one, Lily?"

I nod. "Please. I'm exhausted today."

"Not sleeping well in the old house?" North asks.

I shrug because I can't exactly tell another stranger how I'm a freak and let strangers into my bed. "It's weird living alone . . . I never have before."

"Who did you live with before moving here?"

"My boyfriend, or rather ex-boyfriend, and before that, my mom. Shit, I haven't even told my mom I moved. I wanted to wait until I was here, and I only got the phone connected today."

"Oh no, will she be mad?"

I shake my head. "Maybe mad I didn't tell her, but more she will want to know why Charles and I broke up, and I'm not ready to tell her about that yet."

"You're an adult. Tell her when it feels right."

"Are you ready to order?" Asher asks from behind the counter.

"Can I get the Eggs Benny, extra bacon?" I'm practically salivating just thinking about it.

"You got it," he replies, then looks at North.

"The breakfast burger."

Asher doesn't write the order down; he just disappears out the back.

"Asher doesn't give you a hard time about you and his brother?"

North laughs. "Nah, he tried once, and we got into a fistfight. So, Harlen told you about our situation?"

I nod. "Well, it kind of started as more about him liking things in his ass, which I think he said to piss Asher off and it worked."

"Asher has always struggled to understand our dynamic. It works for us. One day we might find a woman and settle down, but we are in our early twenties, so what's the rush? Anyway, what's the deal with you and your ex? He didn't want to move to the middle of nowhere with you?"

"He doesn't know. We weren't a good fit. I wanted things he didn't, and he made me feel like shit about myself. I don't have to put up with disrespect just because he ticked all the initial boxes."

The door chimes and neither of us turns to see who it is.

"What boxes were they?"

I hold my first finger up. "Good looking." Then the rest of my fingers follow. "Charming, attentive, goal oriented."

"Sounds a bit like me."

North rolls his eyes, and I turn to the man now standing behind us holding his hand out to me. "Tom Morgan, the mayor's grandson, and deputy for Maple Hollow."

"It's nice to meet you, Tom."

Asher thankfully brings out our breakfast and places it down on the counter.

"Thanks for stopping by, Tom. Lily and I are having breakfast," North says.

"Yes, I didn't mean to interrupt. Have a great day, Lily. We should have lunch one day."

"Be sure to invite your wife," Asher says, handing Tom a to-go cup.

"Of course. It would be good for Lily to get in with the right crowd and make some female friends."

Asher walks away, done with the conversation, and Tom waves as he leaves. I give him a small wave back. "So, we don't like Tom?"

"Nope. He bullied Eli throughout high school, and Harlen and I may or may not have slept with all of his girlfriends as payback."

"You did not!" I say with a laugh. "Does he know?"

North nods. "Well, mostly. He thinks his wife was safe because we were older, but she willingly jumped into bed with me before their wedding. I know I'm a terrible person, but I would die for Eli and Harlen. Eli might look big and tough, but his scars are a touchy subject."

"It sounds like Tom wouldn't be faithful either, so they're probably a good match."

North smiles at me, and we chat while we eat breakfast. Once we are done, North tries to pay the bill, but I bump him out of the way, insisting I pay since he is driving me home after I grab groceries, and he unhappily lets me pay.

The grocery store is more like a convenience store, small with just enough to get you by. North lets me know he or Harlen go into Willow Grove once a month to stock up on food and I am welcome to tag along. I decide to ditch the thrift store for today; there is no rush to replace the things I broke. North talks my ear off about the job he is currently doing but stops when we pull up at my house and we get out. He grabs my groceries out of the back of his truck and insists he brings them inside.

"Wow, I didn't realize how run-down this place has gotten over the years. I should check the stairs."

"They seem fine."

He keeps walking to the stairs, then puts all his weight on each one as he ascends. "This one needs to be replaced. I can stop by and do it sometime this week for you."

"Are you sure? I would hate to be a burden. Harlen says you work too hard as it is."

"Harlen worries too much. I only take on what I can do, and I like to stay busy."

I unlock the door and push it open so he can walk inside. He goes straight toward the kitchen as if he has been here before.

"I can't believe it still looks the same. Mavis used to bake us cookies and invite us over—normally she had some odd jobs for us."

I look around, wishing I had some fond memories of my grandmother, beyond the partial memory from when I was a child. Mom never really talked about her—I guess she didn't know her well. My dad was a dick and didn't care about anyone but himself.

"You might need to replace some of these beams too. Why don't I come through and do a full inspection? That way you know what needs to be done over time. There is a scrap yard in Willow Grove, and you can get cheap materials from there, then I can help fix it up."

"I can't ask you to do that, North. You're too generous."

"You are not asking, I'm offering."

"If you're sure, but I will pay you for your time."

North smiles. "If you can make chocolate chip cookies like your grandmother, it's a deal. I'm going to head off, but I will pop back in a few days for the stairs."

"If you insist," I say.

North's gaze snags on the small bowl of knickknacks at one end of the kitchen counter, and he picks up the gifted switchblade I've placed in there. "Where did you get this? It looks handmade."

"A friend left it here."

"Tell them I said nice work." He stares at it a moment longer, then puts it back where he found it.

I walk him to the door and wave as he drives away. I guess one good thing is that I'm making friends. Even if it is with the town outcasts, it feels like it's where I belong.

Once I pack the groceries away, I decide it's time to log into my social media. I have been avoiding all of it since Charles told everyone, and people took it upon themselves to inbox me. Some told me how gross I was, and others sent offensive images and offers to hurt me. As expected, my inbox is full, and I delete most of them without reading them. I hover over the message thread from Charles, deciding to open it.

> Why are you not answering my calls?

> Come on, just talk to me.

> I'm sorry, I shouldn't have told people.
>
> Zoe said you left.

I scan the rest, all variations of what I have already read. I send him one back in the hope he will leave me alone.

> Please stop messaging me. I have left and do not plan to come back. I'm moving on with my life and suggest you do the same. I don't want to talk to you. After shaming me, there is no way our relationship can come back. Instead of talking it through with me, you went to your friends and now everyone knows my deepest and darkest secrets. I have a chance to start over and I plan to do that.

I hit send, then scroll until I find the last message I sent my mom and hit call on the FaceTime icon.

"Hey, sweetheart," she says when her face fills the screen.

"Hey, Mom."

"Are you okay? Charles has been calling me looking for you. I figured you two had a fight and you would call me when you were ready."

I can't help my sigh. Mom has always loved Charles—she said he was a good choice because he comes from a good family, has goals, and would make a good husband. She wanted me to learn from her mistakes and not fall for a small-town boy.

"We broke up. Things didn't work out."

She gasps. "Oh no, what happened?"

"The details don't matter, only that we won't be getting back together. But I also wanted to tell you I dropped out of school."

"Lilybeth May Harper, you did what?!"

I laugh at her full-naming me and trying to pretend she is mad. "It's not a big deal. Do you remember Dad's mother, Mavis? She left her house to me and I'm now in Maple Hollow."

"You moved ten hours away and didn't think to let me know? I love and support you, honey, but I think leaving school is a mistake. However, it's your life and as long as you're happy, that's the main thing. When we get back, I'll come visit, and we can talk about this some more."

"Sounds good, Mom. I love you too. Say hi to Jerry for me."

"I will. I have to go. Be safe and call me soon."

Once we end the call, I see Charles has responded.

> I don't accept this is over. I will give you some more time to come to your senses, but we were good together.

There is no point responding if he refuses to hear me. I won't let him ruin my mood, and he isn't worth my time. Today I plan to box up any of my grandmother's belongings I don't need and donate them to the thrift store, but first I'll pack away my groceries and hunt for her cookbook. Old people normally have one filled with their recipes, right? And if North wants chocolate chip cookies for fixing my house, the least that I can do is try to recreate hers.

Chapter Seven

North

As I pull around to the back of the old hospital building that houses our spacious bachelor pad, I'm greeted by Eli and Harlen, who have both come out to help me unload my truck. I flash them a toothy smile and Harlen raises a brow suspiciously.

"Why the fuck are you so happy?"

I shrug. "It's a good day. I had breakfast with Lily, and get this, Tom tried to hit on her. But she wasn't interested in the slimeball, of course. Oh, and Mavis's old house needs some work."

Harlen smiles back. "So you have a crush on Lily?"

"What? No! She's just good company. It's nice to have someone other than your ugly faces to talk to."

Harlen clutches his chest in affront. "I am not ugly—you take that back."

Eli elbows Harlen and they both look at me. "What? I feel like I'm missing something."

"Let's unload this wood before we tell you."

"Hmm, it wouldn't have anything to do with a certain handmade switchblade being left at Lily's house?" I say as I look at Eli.

I know it's his, but the better question is, why was he there? He never leaves the house, except when he is in the cemetery, and that is usually only at night. Plus, if Lily knew his name, she would have referred to him as Eli, not as a "friend."

Eli's eyes connect with mine, and he looks guilty. Harlen coughs quietly and interrupts our standoff. "Okay, maybe we should do this before we unload. Fine, long story short, Eli was taking part in the Halloween festivities and kind of chased Lily and fucked her in the cemetery."

My gaze locks back on Eli, and he swallows. "Why wouldn't you tell me? And why the fuck are you chasing girls and fucking them in the cemetery? It's illegal to take advantage of someone." Harlen laughs at that. "And I'm glad you think this is funny," I snap. "What if she goes to the sheriff? You want him to go to jail?"

"She consented, calm down. And the second time, it wasn't only Eli. Cute as a button Lily has a kink, which she told me all about at the diner after I was pissed at Asher and blurted out that I like things in my ass. I told her about our situation, and she told me hers."

"So, you what? Chase her and fuck her? How does she not know who you are? She met you."

"We wear Halloween masks. And we sort of

promised her three next time, so you better get on board fast. We would hate to break a promise to a pretty girl."

I scratch my head. I'm down for a lot of things, but this sounds complicated. "She knows the sound of my voice, so it would never work."

"I talk," Eli says, and my jaw drops as I whip my head toward him.

"You talk to her? I feel like I'm in an alternate universe right now. Help me unload the truck so I can process this shit. She really fucked you both, not knowing who you were?"

Eli nods and Harlen can't wipe the shit-eating grin off his face. "She sure did, and she was dripping wet before we even got to that part. Eli did so well—he ate her out and she practically drowned him."

I must admit, knowing Eli talks to her and has fucked her has me curious. Eli doesn't leave the house to meet women, so he got stuck with us by default. Harlen and I usually go to Willow Grove if we need to be with a woman—it's easier than screwing a girl from our town. It's slim pickings around here, and she would expect to wake up with an engagement ring on her finger. I'm surprised a line of mothers with single sons haven't shown up at Lily's house yet with casseroles and tales of their "special" young men.

Despite that imagery making me bristle, it doesn't change the fact that lying to a woman to get her rocks off feels wrong. "What happens when she finds out it's you? Then what? We don't need that kind of heat on us."

Harlen scoffs. "The town has painted us as the bad

guys, though they might tolerate you a little more because you are the nicer one. As for Lily, we can tell her eventually, or not. Either way, a few harmless fucks to show her that her kinks are not a bad thing, like her douche of an ex told her, will make her feel good about herself. If you don't believe us, come watch."

I mull over what he is saying for a minute; could she really want this? It's one thing to role play when you know who is behind the mask, but thinking it is a stranger, then finding out they are people you have met and interacted with, is another thing entirely. It feels like a lie.

"I'll come and watch, but—and a *big* but—if I feel like you're taking advantage of her, I plan on telling her."

"You know I would never take advantage of a woman," Harlen snaps defensively.

"I want to believe that, but it doesn't sound that way."

"Come watch and you will see," Eli says.

I nod once. While I want to believe them, when something sounds too good to be true, it normally is. Like the time Harlen was almost adopted by Agnes's parents with Asher, but on the day they came to pick him up, Eli clung to him. Harlen took Eli's face in his hands and planted a kiss on his lips, and they changed their minds.

Some things are too good to be true.

Harlen was devastated for weeks afterwards to not see Asher every day. At first Asher wanted to come back, but Harlen put on a brave face and told him he wanted to stay with Eli and me. From that day forwards, I swore I would make sure nothing bad ever happened to them. No matter what stupid pranks Harlen convinced Eli to take part in, I was right there watching their backs. And if I need to reveal their identities to Lily before this gets started in order to spare them, then I will.

Days pass, and I still can't get the situation with Lily out of my head. Even when I went back to fix her front stairs, the idea sparked in the back of my mind. How could a sweet girl like her be okay with this? Her kinks don't bother me—it's the stranger aspect. Does she not realize how dangerous what she's doing could be? I guess that plays into it, but what if instead of them she had encountered some perverts? I wouldn't put this past Tom Morgan; his ego would eat this shit up. How cute little Mary Wilkins ended up with him is beyond me—she was a straight-A student in high school with messy hair and one friend. If I remember correctly, Tom bullied her, calling her a nerd every chance he got and would even throw his trash at her.

Harlen lays his head in my lap, while he scrolls through Lily's social media. She's been posting updates on the house, along with her progress in removing Mavis's old things and bringing back to life the stuff she wants to keep.

"Should I go help her? It's hurting my soul to watch her fix that old set of drawers."

The door opens and Eli steps through, shaking his wet hair all over the carpet. We have renovated the entire second floor of the old hospital as our living space, while leaving downstairs still old and run-down. The reason we still do the haunted house every year, though none of us want to admit it, is it's nice the people in town need us for something.

"Where have you been?" Harlen asks him, barely looking up from his screen.

"Just thinking in the cemetery. But then Lily turned up in the rain and is sitting at her grandmother's grave."

That gets Harlen's attention.

"Don't even think about it," I warn.

"Why not?" he whines. "It's perfect. She knows she can say no, and we're not restricted to inside her house. Eli already feels terrible since she broke half her dinner plates throwing them at him last time."

I look over the lounge at Eli and he shrugs.

My curiosity has gotten the better of me. "Fine, but remember, I'm watching."

Harlen jumps from my lap and races down the hall. When he returns, he throws the masks at us. "Let's leave them turned off for a bit and make it known she is being watched first."

Eli nods, and I keep quiet, still skeptical she is okay with this.

All three of us walk toward the cemetery. The newer plots have access via a new road, but Mavis was buried beside her late husband, Frank. She once mentioned she bought the spot next to him knowing when she went, her place was ready and waiting beside him. It's romantic really, especially when you realize Frank died almost two decades ago. I never believed in love until I met that woman. Frank had passed before we met, but Mavis would show us her photo albums and the pure love in her eyes as she told us the stories about their life made me hope that maybe one day I could have that too. But it also cemented the fact that I wouldn't have it without my best friends by my side.

Sure enough, Lily is sitting with her legs crossed in the rain, staring at the two headstones. She doesn't look upset; if anything, she seems happy.

"Let's spread out and force her away from the town up toward the bluff," Harlen whispers, then moves, not waiting for an answer. Eli follows his lead as I stand here and watch.

The light rain sprinkling down is not enough to soak through my hoodie, but Lily has been out here a while, and her hair is now limp around her face. A twig snapping in the distance has her head jolting to the side, and she stares into the darkness. We don't do streetlights here in Maple Hollow unless it's the town square—that place is lit up like a damn Christmas tree all year round.

Her gaze settles back to the headstones in front of her after a few moments, but occasionally she looks up as if she is waiting.

When an owl hoots further in the darkness, she jumps to her feet and pulls her cardigan around her slight frame as she looks over her shoulder. The fear of being alone in a cemetery is kicking in—it's written all over her face. I stay hidden behind the large tree, watching her.

She heads off toward town when Eli's mask illuminates the darkness and her footsteps falter.

He switches it off straight away, and then Harlen's comes to life.

"What are you waiting for?" she screams as she spins in a semicircle so both men can hear her well. Huh, so Harlen and Eli were not full of shit—she really wants this. With that realization, I switch my mask on, and her head whips toward me with a gasp.

"Don't get caught!" Eli yells, and she runs away from the town, deeper into the cemetery.

Tonight could be a lot more fun than I anticipated.

Chapter Eight

Lily

Days have passed since they came to my house and rocked my world. I almost thought maybe they'd given up. When the twig snapped, I thought I was hearing things, and the damn owl genuinely scared the pants off me. Just because I like to be chased doesn't mean I'm immune to things that go bump in the night. But stupidly, I feel safer knowing they are out there, and that they followed through on their promise to bring a third. I wonder what they have planned. By the way they are spaced out, it seems their aim is to hunt me down and push me to run further into the cemetery, away from the edge of town.

My pace isn't overly speedy in the growing darkness, and their masks flash on every now and again to let me know they are still there. My heart beats hard in my chest and a thrill of excitement rushes through my bones. If you asked me six months ago if I would live out my wildest fantasies with a bunch of unknown strangers, I would have laughed. After tonight, I should put an end to it. I have had my fun and now little specks of doubt are creeping into my mind. What if they're married, or biding their time and having fun before they hurt me, so I don't tell anyone? Yet the thrill of it has my legs moving forward. If I try to head in a direction they don't want me to, the masks come on.

It's not until we clear the old cemetery and step onto what the local map calls the bluff—a cliff that drops straight into the ocean below—that all three masks turn on. The rapid beat of my heart picks up as they move toward me. Darting into a clearing in the trees, while the sound of footsteps follows close behind me, I know I want this—I need it. It's the only thing making me feel sane since I uprooted my entire life, my entire future. It is why I was in the cemetery in the first place, talking to Mavis, hoping she would give me a sign I had made the right choice. Would she have thought I was insane for letting strangers chase me and fuck me? What am I thinking? Of course she would. Right now, even I think I am, especially since I'm outnumbered. Yet the depraved side of me keeps dipping and weaving, waiting for the moment they have me right where they want me.

A scream peels from my lips as I smash into a solid body in the darkness. I fall straight back on my ass, and the mask turns on as he steps forward.

"Miss me, baby?"

I scramble backward until a set of boots stops me. I'm

surrounded, though the third masked man stands back a little further than the other two.

"On your knees."

Only one of them talks, so he must be the one in charge. I know he is from the haunted house; his mask is different from the other two. I do as he asks and push up on my knees. The masked stranger behind me hooks his arms under my elbows and rotates me to face the other masked man.

"Show him how good your mouth works."

I nod and lean forward, then with trembling fingers I undo the button on his jeans and pull down the zipper. I'm surprised when his cock pops straight out, not restricted by boxers. Leaning forward, I push up higher onto my knees and lick his shaft from base to tip, causing him to moan deep in his throat. One of them steps up behind me and twists my hair in their hand. It pulls my head back into their crotch, forcing me to look up at them before he pushes my head forward toward his friend's erect cock. I reach out and wrap my hand around the base as the masked man behind me sets the pace, pushing my head down and pulling it back up. Looking up at the masked man in front of me, I see his head is tilted backward.

The man behind me pushes me down, further and further, my gags spurring him on. He pushes me past my normal comfort level, yet I hum around his friend's length, enjoying every damn second.

Little rocks dig into my knees as I get mouth fucked by the stranger. When his cock swells inside my mouth, I brace for what comes next. This used to be the worst part of a blow job, Charles wanting me to swallow, but in this moment, I can't wait to have this man's cum shoot down my throat.

The man behind me pulls me backward just as the saltiness hits my tongue. He yanks down on my hair, so I'm once again forced to look up at him. Then he uses two fingers to push any spilled cum back into my mouth, fucking my mouth with them and making sure I don't waste a drop. Once he removes his fingers, he pushes me down onto all fours and the sound of his zipper echoes around us. The fresh air hits my ass as my linen pants are pulled down my thighs.

The man with the different mask kneels in front of me, and he runs the pad of his thumb over my lips.

"I don't think you're afraid of us anymore, baby," he says. "I think you like being our toy. To chase, to use."

The masked man behind me thrusts into me so deep, it feels like his cock might come out my mouth, which falls open as my hair is pulled once again. "Please use me," I pant as his thrusts get harder.

The man in front of me nods as he gets to his feet. He pulls his own cock from his sweats, before he palms it in his hand, stroking it slowly, and it's almost hypnotizing.

My pussy clamps around the cock fucking me with a vice-like grip as my orgasm explodes through my body. He slows as he lets me ride out the pleasure, and when my arms threaten to give out, a large arm wraps around my stomach, holding me up.

"Eyes up here, baby. Watch as I come all over your pretty face."

I look up, trying to see the eyes behind the mask. I can't, but knowing he can see me is enough as he strokes himself. The girth of this man has me wanting him inside me again, stretching me out.

The world is quiet, the only sounds around us my pants, moans, and screams. I wonder if I will wake up and this entire week will have been nothing but a dream. Back to the reality of missionary in bed, adventurous being if my legs were bent behind my head as if I was an Olympic gymnast.

The man behind me pulls me back hard. His thrusts shorten as he moans his pleasure. He keeps his hips moving through his release, then he pulls out, and I feel the loss instantly.

"Put her back on her hands and knees."

The man to the side hasn't moved in a while and I look over at him. He must take it as permission because he steps beside the main man, and they share a look and nod.

"Keep your eyes on him."

I do as I'm told and look at the man now standing in front of me. He tilts his head and looks down at me, and I wonder what he is thinking. Does he think I'm a dirty whore? Or is he enjoying watching as his friends fuck me?

"Oh, fuck!" I scream, my nails digging into the dirt when a tongue pushes inside me. My eyes roll into the back of my head as his tongue works me over, and he shuffles underneath me. It would be so easy to look back and see who it is, but I do as I'm told and keep my eyes trained on the two men in matching masks standing before me—the one on the left bumps his shoulder into the one on the right. Rough hands grip my waist and pull me down, so almost all my weight is on his face, the roughness of his stubble scratching against my most sensitive area. He uses his hands to rock my hips as I find a steady rhythm, then his grip loosens and I ride his face. The closer I get to an orgasm, the faster I move, no longer caring if I suffocate him between my legs or grind too hard—all I can think about is chasing the high.

"Oh shit, I'm gonna come," I cry out, not caring if the entire world hears me. My body shakes, and I grip the ground, not giving a shit if I have to dig dirt out of my nails for a week. I scream as I arch my back, my orgasm hitting me hard and fast. Every inch of my body tingles as I ride out my release on the eager mouth below me. These men are ruining me for anyone who comes after them.

My arms give out and I collapse to the ground. One of them picks me up, brushing my hair from my face, then cradles me in his arms as he walks back the way we came. My body is spent, and I close my eyes. I know my dreams will be filled with masks and orgasms. I feel small in his arms, but safe. I must fall asleep, because when I wake up, my sheets are filled with dirt and there are no masked men in sight.

Chapter Nine

Harlen

North carries Lily back to our place. She is out cold with her head resting peacefully against his chest. He can't carry her the entire way to her house, so we both get into his truck; I'm behind the wheel, while he keeps her tucked close to his body.

Eli split off somewhere around the cemetery—he won't want to be around for this conversation. He knows North is our voice of reason when neither of us can see straight. I don't speak, and I know North is still processing what just happened. If he tells us what we are doing is wrong, both Eli and I will believe him.

The drive to her house isn't far, and once we pull up out the front, I get out and race up the front porch, lifting the doormat and pulling out her spare key. After I've opened the door, I put the key back where I found it. While it's risky to bring her home without our masks on, it's one we are willing to take. As I told North, I'm not purposefully hiding my identity from Lily, but she literally told me she likes the fact she doesn't know who is chasing her. Besides, it makes it less complicated for her.

North carries her upstairs, and silently I direct him to her room. He raises a brow and I smirk; yes, I know where her room is. I move ahead of him to pull back her comforter, and he places her down on the white sheets, then slips her shoes off and pulls the comforter up, finally tucking a strand of hair behind her ear. He motions toward the door and we both leave her room, closing the front door behind us on our way out. North twists the handle quietly to make sure it's locked.

"I don't see any harm in what you're doing," he says as I slide into the driver's side of the truck once more. "But I think it will complicate your friendship with her when she finds out you are one of the men behind the masks."

"You think so?"

He closes the passenger door and buckles up before answering. "I do. What if she thinks you betrayed her trust by not telling her it was you? For now, it all seems harmless, but consider telling her sooner rather than later."

"Does that mean you will not chase her again?" I ask, my eyes trained on the road as I drive away from my newest craving.

"I don't know. I think I want to pursue her outside of the mask—she's fun to be around. But I might talk to Eli first. He seems very into this whole thing, so I'll also keep that in mind."

North places his hand on my thigh, stroking his fingers along my jeans. My dick gets the memo quickly, and so does North, moving his hand so it sits over my cock.

"Don't fucking tease me. If you want to suck my cock, then do it. You can see how good she tastes."

North undoes my jeans and pulls my cock out. He closes his hand around me, stroking and playing until I'm so hard I could explode in his hand and be satisfied. We hit the back road to the hospital, since any other access is blocked off by the haunted trail bullshit. North undoes his seat belt and repositions his body. He leans over, not wasting any time, and sucks me straight into his mouth. North isn't like Eli. I can't force my length down his throat—he would nut punch me. North does things his own way, stroking me at the base in time with his mouth. I want nothing more than to fist his hair and guide his movements, but I can't because as I pull into the driveway, I narrowly miss the pile of fucking wood he stacked by the back entrance. After parking the truck, I lean my head back against the seat and close my eyes, feeling his mouth sucking and his tongue flat against my shaft. Within a minute, I'm lifting my ass off the seat and coming right down his throat.

North pulls back and wipes his lips on the sleeve of his hoodie. "Her pussy tastes sweet against your cock. I might not take part until she knows, but you better come fuck my mouth after you fuck her."

The back door slams open, and Eli stands silhouetted in the doorframe. "Shit," I mutter. "I'll go talk to him before he gets antsy and does something stupid like setting Tom Morgan's wife's flowers on fire again."

North smirks. "I'm going to shower and go to bed. I promised Lily we would go to the hardware store together tomorrow."

I slide from the truck and head toward Eli. We have different dynamics; there is Eli and me, and North and me. While I know North has fucked Eli once before, they rarely do anything unless we are all together, and that hasn't happened in a very long time.

Eli turns to walk inside, and I run up behind him and jump onto his back, wrapping my arms lightly around his neck. He walks us up into the shower in his room. We don't shut doors often. If North joins us, then so be it—but he won't. I heard his door click shut, and that is where he will stay until he leaves bright and early tomorrow morning.

Eli shucks me off his back. I strip down naked while he turns on the water, and he holds his hand under the stream until it's the right temperature.

"Is he going to make us stop?" Eli asks, his back turned to me. Stepping up behind him, I wrap my arms around his middle. Grabbing at the hem of his shirt, I pull it up and over his head.

"No, but he thinks we should tell her. Especially if we plan to be her friend."

"Why would she want to be friends with me? Girls pity me." He spins around to face me.

"They do not. You are fucking hot, Eli James. So hot it's hard to fathom having to share you with her. I hope you don't forget who you belong to." I slide my hands down his abs, and he shivers under my touch.

"I will always belong to you, Harlen Cooper, but there is something about Lily and I don't want to let that go."

"And I would never ask you to. But you should give her a chance to get to know you. Come with us one day—when you're ready."

"People in town will stare," he mutters as he drops his pants to the ground and steps into the shower, with me right behind him.

"Who cares if they do?! Fuck them, Eli. We're allowed to be happy. I don't care what anyone thinks besides you and North."

He picks up the body wash and squirts it onto his hands, then rubs his palms over my chest. "They all hate me on behalf of your brother."

I snort. "And don't forget how gay you are as well."

That makes him smile. This backward-ass town hates three men living together, and it doesn't help how I flaunt the fact that I'm fucking them both in everyone's faces just to make them uncomfortable. But only if they say something to me first.

"Also, don't worry, Tom has made it his personal mission to warn Lily away from us. The poor guy doesn't know how to take a hint and Lily is too nice to tell him to fuck off."

"Fuck, I hate that guy. I don't know why he got

married when he still constantly hits on women," Eli grumbles.

North and I see it all the time, normally when people from Willow Grove come for celebrations, as Maple Hollow goes all out for every occasion—not only the big ones.

After Halloween, the town square gets ready for Maple Hollow's annual cooking competition. It doesn't sound like a big deal, but the men drag out smokers and families compete against families. Then we jump straight into Thanksgiving decorations.

Once we finish in the shower and dry off, Eli drags me into his bed and wraps me in his arms. Some nights, he likes to share a bed, usually when he is feeling insecure.

"Do you think she would like me if she knew who I was?"

Rolling over to face him, I nod my head. "She doesn't seem like the type who would care, Eli. We talk about you all the time, and she asks me how you are. She knows you don't like to leave the house much and how you don't talk unless you want to. You really should come with us to hang out with her one day."

"Maybe. Do you wonder if she could be the one we are missing? I know North really wants a girl around."

"She could be, if we told her who we are. If we don't, then eventually she will meet someone and what we have will taper off into a distant memory."

The thought makes my stomach twist into knots. Is it possible to like someone this quickly and not simply because she lets us chase her? The more I get to know her, the more I enjoy being around her. Maybe North is on to something. But until Eli is ready, I won't tell her. There is no way I would betray his trust, and neither would North.

Chapter Ten

Lily

Tonight is officially Halloween. North told me earlier to enjoy the spooky vibes, because come morning, the entire town will be packed up as if nothing ever happened, and the town square will be ready for the cook-off. Apparently, a lady named Anabelle wins the bake-off every year with her famous blueberry pie, and Samuel and Joel go head-to-head with their smoked meat. If I'm being honest, I'm excited to buy some of the food, which they sell at the end of every day after the judges get their portion.

As I walk through the town square, I see kids trick-or-treating. I managed to find a set of angel wings at the thrift store, and I knew they would go perfectly with the sexy little white dress I'm rocking that I bought ages ago to wear to a sorority party.

"Lily," a voice calls from behind, and I turn to see a short woman chasing me. She stops next to me and puts her hands on her knees. "You're fast for a woman in heels."

I smile at her. She looks like she dressed up as Mrs. Potts from *Beauty and the Beast*. "Sorry, I didn't hear you until just now."

"That's okay, I haven't had the chance to introduce myself yet. I'm Mrs. Morgan, and my husband is the mayor. We wanted to ask if you'd like to be a judge at the upcoming cook-off. We took a vote at the town meeting, and everyone thinks you would be perfect. You have no history with the winners and would be a fresh slate."

"Oh, I would love to," I reply. Since I plan on staying, I should get a little more involved. "And there was a town meeting?"

"Yes, dear. We have them on the last Monday of every month. Everyone is welcome to attend. My grandson Tom was supposed to invite you along. I guess the boy forgot."

"I guess so. What do I need to do to be a judge?"

"Oh, that's easy. Every night this week at six, the judges sample each entrant's food and give it a score. Then on Saturday the top three in each category battle it out and winners are announced."

"I can do that, Mrs. Morgan. I will see you tomorrow night."

She smiles and waves at me as I wander off around the town square. I watch the children run around to each stall, while parents chase some of the smaller children through the mazes. I really love how they have everything set up here; there's an overwhelming sense of community spirit.

The line to the cotton candy has gone down and I quickly join the end. A group of high school aged girls are huddled in front of me, and I can't help but overhear their conversation.

"Come on, Betty. We all signed up for the hide-and-seek. Rumor has it that Harlen will be one of those seeking tonight, and how hot is he?!"

"Seriously, Melody, you really think someone like Harlen would want a high school girl?"

"You know they're all together, right? They don't even like girls."

"My mom told my aunt they only want one girl to, you know, share. Could you imagine being the meat in that man sandwich?"

"Don't be a wuss. We are finally old enough to go this year. Someone should ask Michael to meet us at eight—the line will be too long if we wait."

The girls keep arguing about this hide-and-seek game, and I wonder if I should go. Hopefully, my masked man will be there—he was the first time. Once I get my cotton candy, I move away and pull out my phone. Seeing I have unread messages from Zoe and Charles on my social media, I open Zoe's first.

> Thanksgiving, have a bed ready. I'm coming to visit.

Excitement fills my soul. I've missed my best friend so much. She was the only good thing in my life for such a long time. She was the only person to befriend the new girl, even if she was a nerd.

> Squee! Can't wait to show you around.

My stomach churns as I open the message from Charles. I know I should block him, but deep down, I want him to see how happy I am now.

> Didn't take you long to move on. Please talk to me, I want to say sorry.

Anger takes over, and I furiously type back a response.

> What I do is none of your business. Please stop, or I will be forced to block you.

Apart from those two sentences, I stop responding. He can't force me to do anything I don't want to do, just like I couldn't make him do what he didn't want to do, but at the very least, I won't plaster it over social media for all our friends to see.

With nothing left to do in the town square, I head toward the old hospital where the hide-and-seek is going to happen. Let's hope my masked man is watching and gives me one last night to remember. With Halloween officially over tomorrow, I know this will be the last chance where the masks will not look out of place. Who knows? Maybe next year they will pick up where they left off. A girl can only dream.

A young girl sits at the sign-up table and smiles warmly as I approach.

"Welcome to the biggest game of hide-and-seek. If you signed up to seek, you will need to head to the other table."

"Um, I would like to hide," I tell her.

"That is amazing. Write your name on the sheet, then you have five minutes to hide before we let in the seekers. You can hide inside on the lower level of the building, or out through the cemetery if you dare, just stay inside the marked-off areas. Once you've been found, you are to come back out and mark your name off. If you are not found within twenty minutes, a siren will sound, and you can come out of hiding. If there is more than one person not found, you will be eligible to go into the final round and be in the running for the grand prize, which is a thousand dollars in cash, a dinner for two at Elsie's in Willow Grove, and a night at the Firefly Inn."

I scribble my name on the sheet as she hands me a wrist band and tells me to line up at the doorway with the others. I see the girls from earlier, and they watch me and whisper as I approach.

"Okay, everybody, we have our first hiders. We will let them in, and they get five minutes to hide. Then they'll hear this sound," an older man says, hitting a horn which blares so loudly my ears ring. "Once that siren goes, the seekers will enter. They have twenty minutes to find you all. When you hear the siren again, if you are not found, please come out and get your name marked off so we can start the second round. Good luck."

We are all let through, and the girls giggle and run ahead, leaving me. Instantly I can feel eyes on me. At first, I wonder if it's just my mind playing tricks, like last time in the hall with all the cloaked figures where one jumped out. Moving into the building and through the maze of rooms, I look for somewhere to hide. I walk into a room filled with hay bales and large pumpkins carved to look scary. I'm hunting around to find the perfect spot when the horn blares—shit, I ran out of time. There is a small gap between a hay bale and the wall, so I wedge my body in there nice and tight. The wait has my heartbeat picking up at the sound of footsteps and screams, and after a few minutes the door opens and I wiggle myself down as flat as possible, except I hear the door lock engage. Moving so I can peek over the hay bale, I glimpse two masked men standing by the door before I duck down.

"Were you waiting for us, baby?" The husky voice comes from much closer now, and like an idiot, I squeak and drop down further. "How about we play a game? You run, and if we catch you, we'll fill both your holes."

"What happens if I don't get caught?" I whimper from behind the safety of the hay bail.

"We know where you live, and your ass is safe."

The thrill of excitement makes me want to be caught. I have been preparing myself for this, wanting to take two of them at the same time. Thankfully, after I told Zoe what happened with Charles, she went on a sex toy shopping spree for me—that girl is a huge advocate for self-care. Billy the butt plug was a gift that keeps on giving.

They locked the door behind them, so it means the only exit is the secondary door. I pop up and sprint toward it.

"Catch me if you can," I say as I twist the handle and run through.

The adjoining room leads out into a maze with walls at least eight feet tall and made from hay bales. I twist and weave through them, but it's so dark in here. I hit a dead end and turn back, making it just in time to hit another part of the maze and run for cover. Footsteps fall close behind me and drive me further into the maze. Pushing myself to go faster, I run out into an open area. There I stumble across a zombie-looking scarecrow, and I set the light effects off. Its spooky laughter echoes all around me, then my gaze snags on one of the masked men as he steps out from the path I just came from. I back up as he gets closer until I hit a wall of muscle, and an arm wraps around me.

"Found you," he rasps in my ear. "Now be a good girl and close your eyes."

My eyes clamp shut, and I feel him tie a blindfold around my head. The second body comes closer, and his hands fall to my waist. He lifts me and throws me over his shoulder like I'm a rag doll, his hand coming down hard on my ass.

They walk in silence, and while I know I could fight and pretend I don't want to be here, who am I kidding? The chase is fun, but being caught is even better. I'm here for whatever they have planned—even if I'm a little bummed there are only two of them tonight.

The siren goes off and I panic. They will come looking and find me like this. As I try to slide down from his body, I realize it's one thing to do this when no one else knows, but if the town finds out, I would be shunned. I don't want to move again—I like it here. In the time I've been here, I've made friends, and now I feel at peace for the first time in a long time.

"I have to sign off that I'm out. Let me go."

The man beside me chuckles. "No one is looking for you, Lily. Not a single soul. You could vanish and there would be no trace of you here tonight."

"You don't understand," I say as I'm set down on my feet and the sound of a door locking comes from behind me. "I wrote my name on the sheet."

"I took care of it. Now stop talking or I will fill your mouth with my cock." His voice sends a shiver down my spine as fingers grip my dress and hike it up around my waist. "Tell me you went bare under here for me, baby."

At my subtle nod, he groans and runs a finger along my slit, parting my lips as a second body steps up behind me and kisses my shoulder. I gasp—they have their masks off. I could remove the blindfold so easily and see who they are, but then the illusion of this would be gone. One of my shoulder straps falls, and then a hand does the same to the other side. It releases my breasts, and the entire dress is now bunched around my middle. The angel wings are long gone, left in the room where I was hiding.

"We're going to fuck you at the same time and fill you so good you will remember this night forever."

My body trembles under their touch. One pushes his fingers inside me, curling them just right, and every time he slides across my G-spot, my body spasms involuntarily. The other places featherlight kisses on my neck, while rolling my nipples between the pads of his fingers.

The intense pleasure of my G-spot being stimulated has my knees buckling. My body falls forward, and I use the solid wall of man fingering me to hold myself upright as my orgasm hits like a freight train at full speed.

Having my eyes blindfolded heightens every touch, along with every sound. Giving myself to these strangers has been a thrilling experience. I'm trusting people I don't know with my body, yet never once have I felt unsafe. A tear prickles in my eye when I realize these strangers respect my need to explore what I like, but my boyfriend of a year wouldn't even consider it.

A cap opens, and the distinct sound of liquid squirting has my temperature rising. The anticipation of experiencing two men at once has my core wanting more.

"Don't be scared. If it's too much, just say stop."

"Okay, but please don't stop. I want this."

The cold liquid is smeared down my crack and two fingers press against my ass. The man behind me grips my hip firmly with his free hand as he slowly pushes into my tight hole with his lubed digits. Initially, everything in me screams that this feels wrong, but the man in front circles my clit and my body gradually relaxes. As the fingers at the back move faster, a third is added to stretch me out, and my clit is worked with more speed and pressure. My second orgasm isn't as intense, but hits quickly, and my legs still give out. The man in front of me catches me, lifting me up.

"Wrap your legs around my waist."

I do what he asks, and the man behind me squirts the lube again. This time he must rub it on himself, though I tense when I feel the man in front of me move his hands to the sides of my ass cheeks and spreads them as the man behind me rubs his cock along my crack.

"Just breathe," he rasps, and my body tingles from the sound of his husky voice. The head of the other man's cock pushes against my ass. He goes slow, and it burns, but not as much as I expected. It could be because he primed me well with his fingers, and I'm no stranger to a butt plug. As he pushes past the ring of muscles, I breathe and try not to tense.

"Look at you taking his cock in your ass. You are so perfect, baby."

The men sandwich me between them. Their hands shift so the one behind me is now holding my ass, and the other my legs. They move me up and down, making sure I'm well and truly ready to take them both. I throw one arm over the man behind me and use the other to find the massive cock pressed between me and the man in front, and I guide it toward my pussy. When the head is in, I move my hand up to his shoulder and wait as he slowly pushes himself in, inch by inch. I'm so full I don't know how I can take any more, but the second they move, my body thrashes.

"Oh fuck! I feel like you're both in my stomach. Yes!"

We all fall into a rhythm, and my cries of pleasure are

louder than any I have ever made. We are a mess of hands and sweat. I soon forget about the fullness, and as we all move as one, my body becomes lost to the multitude of sensations. The feeling of both their cocks moving at the same pace, the stubble of one of their faces pressed against mine, the breath of the man behind me as he leans over my shoulder and gently blows against my nipple.

"Fuck, I'm going to come," I gasp out between my panting breaths as every nerve ending in my body is ready to fire.

Both men pick up their pace. My head falls back, and my muscles clamp down around them. I scream through my release as my entire body jerks and trembles uncontrollably. The man behind me digs his fingers into my butt cheek so hard I will have crescent-shaped bruises tomorrow. He grunts and stills as his cock pulses in my ass, and after a few moments, he steps back, slowly removing himself. But he doesn't walk away like I expect. Instead, he pulls me so my back rests against his front and his arms are wrapped underneath mine.

"Holy fuck," I whimper out as the movement starts again. My entire body is spent.

"Your cunt looks perfect milking my cock, strangling it."

The man still sheathed in me thrusts deep, my lifeless body taking everything he gives to me. "Touch yourself," he demands.

"I can't," I mumble.

"I can fuck all night, baby. One more orgasm and I will let you finish."

I muster up enough energy to do as he asks, sliding my shaky fingers down my stomach until I find my clit and slowly circle it, sending a shock wave of pleasure shooting through me. It's almost too painful to continue.

"What a good fucking girl, touching yourself for me. Wet your fingers some more and slide them in with my cock."

He stops thrusting, and I move my hand downward. My fingers touch the base of his cock, and a deep rumble from his throat spurs me on. I push my fingers inside myself, rubbing them against his cock and then slide them back out slowly, moving my juices up my pussy, and working myself closer to another orgasm. I move my fingers at the same pace he thrusts, and I whimper as I feel another orgasm building.

"Don't stop," he growls. "You're so close. Let your little cunt strangle me."

With the sound of his voice and those sinful words, my pussy walls spasm and clamp down around him. My voice is now hoarse, but I strangle out one last scream of pleasure as my back arches and I go limp in their arms. If there is such a thing as death via orgasm, this would be how I want to die—flushed, sweaty, and sated.

Passing out in their arms is becoming a habit. I don't know if I could walk even if I wanted to. Let them kill me now—at least I would go out happy. My eyes are heavy as I'm passed to the other man and cradled in his arms.

"Shhh. Sleep, baby. I will take care of you." It is the last thing I hear before I am completely pulled under.

Chapter Eleven

Eli

Following Lily has become an obsession. She never notices me, but I make sure I keep out of sight. The people in town sure as shit notice me, and they whisper among themselves. Some haven't seen me in years, some think I died, while others spread wild lies.

I watch as she gets stopped by almost everyone she walks past, including Tom Morgan. It's all I can do to not step out from behind a smoker when he touches her arm. How dare he touch her! She belongs to us, even if she doesn't know it yet. I'm jealous that North is fixing her house; he has been there every day this week, even giving up a paying job so he can help her. And Harlen has been showing up to help her learn how to restore furniture properly. But me, I hide in the shadows like a chickenshit. Harlen and North both invited me along. They told her I don't like to talk, and they don't think she would judge me, but the step of officially meeting her scares the shit out of me.

She pulls her arm away from Tom and smiles at him politely while pointing to the diner. Thankfully, he lets her go, and I watch as she crosses the street and pulls the door to the diner open.

I cross the street behind her and keep my hoodie pulled all the way up, hoping to conceal my face as much as possible. The chatter in the diner dulls as I step through the door, and all eyes turn to me, except Lily, who sits at the counter with her back to the door. I wish everyone else would do the same. I sneer at Mrs. Bridges, who openly stares at me with her mouth agape, the silly old bat. No doubt the news of me appearing in town will spread like wildfire as soon as she steps foot out that door. I take a seat beside Lily as Asher comes out from the back, and his steps falter when he sees me. It's not that he is shocked to see me out and about, but more because he hates me since I'm the reason his brother wasn't adopted. He doesn't understand the bond we have—it's beyond a typical relationship between two people. Harlen gets me, and he's the reason I wake up every day. I didn't want to after my accident—I wished for death—but having him by my side has kept me strong.

"Eli," he greets me, and that gets Lily's attention. She turns her big blue eyes toward me and smiles, and my lips pull up at the corners.

"Hi, I'm Lily. Harlen and North have told me so much about you. Harlen maybe a little too much."

She holds her hand out toward me, and I take it in

mine with a firm grip, electricity sizzling between us. I want to sit here and have a conversation with her—that is a first for me. Ever since we met, I've loved the way she looks at me when she hears my voice. Though, if I say anything now, it will ruin our secret. And I don't want that, for her or me.

"Harlen was right—he described you so well. Do you want to have breakfast with me? We can move to a table."

I'm nodding before I even realize what I'm doing.

"Can I take your order before you run away?" Asher says. "The usual for you, Lily?" She nods and Asher looks my way.

"I'll get us a table while you decide," she says, placing her hand on my arm as she gets up.

I feel Asher's eyes boring into me as I watch her walk away before turning back to him.

"Leave that girl alone," he says in a low voice. "She is a good girl and doesn't need—"

"Need what?" I growl, and his eyes widen. Asher hasn't heard me talk since we were kids. "Why don't you mind your own fucking business and stay in your lane with your wife? I will have whatever she's having."

With that, I stand and walk over to the table Lily has chosen. Thankfully, it's in the corner, out of Asher's eyesight, and I figured I would order what Lily is having so he can't spit in my food.

She looks up at me and smiles as I sit. It lights up her entire face, and I want to do more to make her smile, just so I can feel this way all day.

"So, Harlen told me you don't really talk. If it's okay

with you, we can use messenger, or I have a notepad in my bag."

Pulling out my phone, I open my social media. I only have two friends—Harlen and North—and I'd swear it's pointless, but since this stupid town works only off Wi-Fi, it's the easiest way to message people. I place it on the table and skate it her way. She picks it up and slides her finger across my screen. There is no passcode since the two people I live with can do what they please with it—I only use it to contact them. She smiles when she takes in my profile picture. It's Harlen, North, and me when we were about sixteen.

"Oh my gosh, look at how cute you all were," she gushes.

She finds her profile and hands it back to me, and the electricity that passes between us when her fingers touch mine is a novel sensation. I feel good and safe when the guys touch me, but this is new and exciting.

She sighs, and I send her a friend request, then open a message thread.

> Are you okay?

She smiles at my message. "Yeah, ex-boyfriend problems. He won't stop messaging me or take no for an answer. I know I should block him, but then it means that chapter of my life is really over. Is it weird that I want him to see how good I'm doing? I think he is jealous of the pictures I've posted of Harlen and North."

She chuckles at the last comment as anger and jealousy course through my veins. Anger that her ex won't leave her alone, and jealousy over her not having a picture of me, though fucking no one would actually be jealous if she posted my photo.

I type another message.

> North and Harlen are nice to look at.

She laughs this time and nods. "They really are. They make it hard to work some days. You're always welcome to come over as well. I wouldn't complain about three hot men working shirtless in the house. Oh shit, was that rude? I know you don't leave the house much, Harlen somewhat filled me in. I say fuck the town and their small-minded thinking. What you guys do in your own home is your business."

> It's not that simple. They all hate me. But I would love to come and help at your place.

"Look what the cat dragged in."

The hairs on the back of my neck stand on end. Tom fucking Morgan, the bane of my existence, and the guy who made high school a nightmare.

"Do you need something, Tom?" Lily asks in annoyance.

He places his hand on her shoulder, and I ball my hands into fists.

"I didn't realize you were friends with Eli. Someone should have warned you about the company you keep."

Lily smiles sweetly up at him and pushes his hand away from her. "Well, luckily, I have no intention of being friends with you. Since we've met, you have made me feel uncomfortable. You never take no for an answer, and you are being rude to my friend. I think you should go."

I snort, and Tom's eyes cut to mine, his glare of hatred aimed right at me. "You really think you have a shot with any of them?" Tom spews, moving his gaze back to Lily. "They all live in sin, or did they not tell you?"

Lily laughs. "They told me, and I hate to break it to you, but women can be friends with men and vice versa without being sleazy. What they do is none of my business. But hey, I should add it to my list of kinks: screwing strangers in public, check, being chased, check, watch three hot men get it on, unchecked."

Laughter spills out of me, something I haven't done in so long, as Tom stares open-mouthed at Lily. Asher's timing is perfect as he arrives at the table and puts our food down.

"Are you good?" Asher asks Tom.

"No, what is happening to our town? First, we have to deal with the gays, and now this woman is promiscuous."

Lily snorts. "Oh no, I'm a lady of the night. Lock up your husbands."

Tom huffs and walks away as Lily chuckles. Asher raises a brow and I just smirk.

"You shouldn't piss him off. He will target you, and

being a deputy has given him a bigger head than he had back in high school—and it was plenty big back then."

"Then he should know better than to make a woman feel uncomfortable and how to keep his hands to himself. If standing up for people's rights pisses him off, then he can arrest me."

"Hey, I'm only trying to look out for you. Tom is a sleazebag and always has been."

"Thanks for the concern, but I'll be fine."

Asher goes back to serving customers. The whispers are not as loud in here, but they all notice me. I wonder what the papers will print tomorrow?

We both eat in silence, and once we are done, Lily looks up. "Did you want to come to the house? North should be there by now; he went to get some supplies from Willow Grove."

I bite my bottom lip. Do I want to go? Yes, but every time she asks me a question, I want to answer her. Would it really be so bad if she knew it was us? Things wouldn't have to change. I would still chase her until her legs gave out, if that's what she wanted. North might be right about this one. Not telling her who we are might not be lying, but sitting with her now and being friendly, it's starting to not hit the same. She thinks this is the first time we have met, but it's not. I follow her everywhere like an obsession. The last one of those I had was Harlen, and I still haven't shaken him all these years later. While I like North a lot, he and Harlen are closer. It's a weird dynamic, but it works for us, and nothing would ever come between the three of us.

When I nod, she claps her hands. "Yay, I think we are going to be good friends."

I have never been good friends with a girl, and I think I might like it. She smells so nice, a lot nicer than Harlen and North.

Chapter Twelve

Lily

Eli tags along with me to the thrift store, where I find some nice jeans to replace the ones I ruined. My mood has been sour since my masked men have been quiet, and I wonder if that ship has now sailed. They had their fun and now are done with me. On the upside, I have been spending a lot of time with Harlen and North, and they have made moving to a new town fun.

The second we turn the corner into my street, I smile at seeing both Harlen and North in my front yard, cutting wood. As we get closer, Harlen turns his head like he can sense our presence—or maybe Eli's. He has told me how he and Eli share a bond he can't quite explain. Harlen slaps North on the arm, and he, too, turns to watch us walking down the street.

I smile at them and, without thinking, take Eli's hand in mine as I drag him down the street. "Look who I found," I shout. "He couldn't resist my charm, so I asked him to come hang out with us. Oh, and I'm firmly on the 'I hate Tom Morgan' bandwagon. The guy's an asshole. Would you believe he tried to warn me away from Eli? Look at him, he is a big teddy bear . . . well, a muscly teddy bear."

"Lucky for us—we could use an extra set of hands," Harlen jokes. "North keeps bossing me around and I would prefer to finish the entry table."

"You boys can get to work, and I will bake the cookies and bring them out when they are ready. And some lemonade. I'm working through Mavis's cookbook. I'm pretty sure I've nailed the cookies now, or at least they're getting better."

North chuckles. "They are definitely getting better."

I leave the guys outside and head indoors, taking the clothes bags straight to the washing machine and dumping them in after removing the tags. Once that is done, I hurry to the kitchen and remove the cookie dough from the fridge. After portioning it all out onto a lined pan, I pop the tray of deliciousness into the oven. I may have cheated and made an extra-large batch yesterday, but I'm determined to get them right.

While they cook, I run upstairs and get changed into a pair of denim shorts and a bikini top. Today it is unusually warm, and I was hoping to convince the guys to take me to the swimming hole they talk so much about. The oven buzzer goes off, and I head back downstairs. The cookies smell amazing as I remove the tray from the oven. I reduced the cooking time slightly from yesterday, and while I don't want to talk too soon, I think this batch might be the one.

After placing the cookies on a plate, I get the pitcher of lemonade out of the fridge and a handful of metal cups from the cupboard, which look like they are from the eighties. I still haven't had the strength to rearrange the kitchen; it feels wrong to remove Mavis from every part of the house.

Once I open the front screen door, three sets of eyes spring to me and goosebumps line my skin under their scrutiny, but damn it feels good to feel sexy.

"Cookies are ready," I say, and they put down their tools.

Eli has pulled his hoodie off, and the man is ripped. Though the scars on his neck are visible, if he removed his shirt, no one would see past his sculpted torso. It's hard to tear my gaze away from him, and he must feel the same way about me because his dark-brown eyes remain locked with mine.

"Wow, get a room you two, but invite me please," Harlen jokes.

Blinking a few times, I shake off the comment and place the cookies and lemonade on the outdoor table which Harlen made me earlier in the week. The three of them climb the new stairs and join me.

"So I was thinking, if you guys have time, could you show me the swimming hole you were telling me about? We don't have many nice days like this left before it gets cold."

"If you're wearing that, I'm in," North says, and as I look over at him, he winks.

God damn my ovaries—North is a very attractive man. He is the tallest of the three, with broad shoulders and a slim waist, whereas Eli is almost as tall, but he is a brick wall of a man. He is solid muscle everywhere. Harlen is the slimmest of them all, and his abs are less defined, but still there.

"Can we take a picture?" I ask. North and Harlen jump straight in. I look over at Eli, giving him a second to decide. "You don't have to if you don't feel comfortable, but trust me when I say you are drop-dead gorgeous, Eli. My college friends will be so jealous."

Eli takes a deep breath and smiles as he steps into the photo. Harlen wraps his arm around his friend and pulls him in closer. Just as we snap the picture, the sound of music blaring catches our attention, and when I turn around, I freeze. Only one person I know would drive a car like that. It pulls up to the curb behind North's truck, and Charles steps out. He always looks so put together in his slacks and polo shirt. Today he wears a sweater knotted over the top, even though it's way too warm. But he makes it work, like he always did.

All three guys follow me down the stairs, and Charles's eyes roam over each of them. Not that he would ever feel intimidated—that is not how he was raised.

"Lily, it's nice to see you."

"Why are you here, Charles? I told you I was done."

Charles grins at me, his dimples on full display. His

charm may have worked once upon a time, but now I can see through the act. "We need to talk. We can't just end a year-long relationship that way."

I feel the guys behind me, and someone's hand rests on my lower back, granting me strength. "But it ended, Charles, the second you shamed me. You might not enjoy the same things sexually as I do, but you were not even willing to talk about it. So now I have nothing left to say to you."

"I said I was sorry—you just threw me off-kilter for a moment. I want to make it work, but I think we should talk about this inside, alone."

"She isn't going anywhere with you."

My eyes widen—that voice.

I turn around and face Eli. "It's you," I whisper.

He nods, sadness deep in his gaze. I don't know why he looks sad, but I jump into his arms and smash my lips to his, one hand firmly on either side of his face as he holds me tightly to him. Hopefully, Charles gets the message loud and clear.

"Wow, it didn't take you long. Maybe everyone was right about you being a whore. I can't believe I wasted a flight to come here to fix us when you're already fucking someone else."

"Three, actually," I say as I pull back from Eli. He slides me down his body, and I turn to face Charles.

"I would probably walk away if I were you," Harlen snarks with laughter in his tone. "Eli likes to use his fists over his words."

Charles scoffs. "I'm staying at the Firefly Inn. If you

come to your senses, I would like it if you had dinner with me."

Charles walks backward, but Eli angles himself in front of me and blocks me from his view. My heart runs rampant in my chest when Eli finally turns around after Charles speeds off. Then I stare at all three of them. "I think we need to talk."

"I think so," North replies.

"How about I pack a picnic and we can go to the water hole and discuss things there?"

They all nod and I walk back inside. I will let them think I'm mad—which I'm not. However, I want them to explain themselves. They don't seem like the types who would have an ulterior motive for what happened between us, but I would like to hear it from them.

After I make us some ham, cheese, and veggie subs, then pack them into an old wicker basket with some other snacks and four bottles of water, Harlen appears in the kitchen and holds his hand out for the basket. He doesn't say anything, just follows me into the living area where I grab four towels off the clean pile destined for the linen cupboard.

In silence we pile into North's dual cab truck—North and Eli in the front, while Harlen gets in the back beside me. North turns on the stereo and some pop song lightly plays in the background as he drives toward Willow Grove. After fifteen minutes, he turns off onto a dirt road, and for at least another five minutes, there is nothing but trees. Then he turns to the right and pulls up in front of a small lake. It has a simple wooden dock that overlooks the water, and a rope hangs from a large tree. This place would be amazing in summer, and I can't wait to come back and sunbathe.

We all pile out of the truck, and Eli gets the towels while Harlen takes the basket, then we set up our picnic on the dock.

"Oh god! The silence is killing me. Please just yell at us or something," Harlen moans.

Honestly, I was wondering who would break first. "I'm not mad at you—I just want to understand how we got here."

Harlen goes to open his mouth, but Eli stops him.

"Please, let me explain." Eli is seated, but still spins me around to face him. "I don't normally talk much. I fear people making fun of me. But when I spoke to you in the haunted house, the way your body reacted made me feel things I have never felt before. That's why I chased you. We never intended to deceive you. But after you told Harlen how you liked being chased by strangers, we didn't want to ruin it for you. And since we are telling the truth," he says, swallowing loudly, "I like to watch you. Not like a creep while you're asleep or anything, but when you go into town. It's been years since I wandered into town, but I can't stay away from you."

"None of us can," Harlen adds.

"For the record, I wanted to tell you," North says.

I look away from Eli and out over the water as I feel my cheeks heat with embarrassment. "What does this mean for our time with the masks?" I whisper.

This is the reason I wanted it to be with strangers. I

feel so much shame about what I like. And for those brief moments, they made me feel like I had nothing to be ashamed of.

Eli wraps his hands around my hips, pulling me into his lap, then grabs my chin so I'm forced to look at him. "This means not only can we chase you with the masks on, but if you want, you can watch us too."

I know exactly what he means. Earlier, in front of Tom at the diner, I made a comment about watching them together being something I would be interested in.

"What is she watching?" Harlen asks. "I think I'm missing something."

Eli smirks. "Lily wants to watch me suck your cock."

My eyes widen, and Harlen leans forward, running his finger down my shoulder blade. "Would you like that?"

I nod.

"Use your words, trouble," North adds.

"Yes, I would like that."

"Never be embarrassed to tell us what you might like, or what you need. We would never make you feel the way your ex did." North grabs me by the hips and pulls me out of Eli's lap. "I think you need to show our girl just how well you can take Harlen's cock."

Harlen stands, grabbing the back of his shirt and pulling it over his head, while North sits me between his open legs, his hand resting on my stomach. Eli gets on his knees and undoes Harlen's jeans, sliding them to the ground. I lick my lips in anticipation, my heart pounding in my chest. North's fingers tease the waistband of my shorts as Eli spits on Harlen's cock. I don't know why that is so sexy, but it sends a thrill of pleasure straight between my legs.

"Wrap those lips around my cock and show the pretty girl how well your throat works."

Harlen's fingers twist in Eli's hair, and I watch as he wraps his luscious lips around the head of his cock, my mouth practically watering when he slides down to the base.

"Do you like that?" North whispers in my ear, and I nod. "I think I should find out for myself."

He dips his hand beneath my bikini bottoms, his fingers running through my slit before they land on my clit. The slow circles North rubs make me whimper, and Eli looks my way, while Harlen thrusts deep in his throat.

"Eyes on me," Harlen demands. "You don't get to look away from me while I'm fucking your throat. This mouth belongs to me."

Harlen's words have me spasming around North's fingers as he pushes them inside me. "Knowing it's us changes nothing, trouble."

North's fingers stroke my internal walls, slowly caressing as we watch Harlen throat fuck Eli. "What a good boy choking on my cock, putting on a show for our girl. Lily, remove your shorts so Eli can see how wet he is making you."

Shimmying my shorts and bikini bottoms down, I kick them off and let my knees fall open. "So fucking perfect and pink. Look how needy her pussy is. Taste her, North, and tell Eli how good she tastes."

North pulls his fingers out of me and brings them to his lips, sucking my juices off his digits, humming as he does. "So damn sweet, Eli," North groans out.

"Do you want to taste her?" Harlen asks, and Eli nods around Harlen's cock. "Then go eat her needy cunt until she creams all over your face."

Harlen pulls back and Eli turns to face me. His eyes dip to my pussy and he licks his lips as he gets to his feet. He moves right in front of me, dropping to his knees, then lies on his stomach, his head moving straight to my pussy, his tongue sweeping the entire length of my slit. Harlen moves to stand over us, his length now in hand as he strokes himself above us, and North remains behind me, his hands cupping my breasts.

"Look at how perfect for us you are, Lily. You couldn't be more in tune with our needs."

I buck up as Eli sucks my clit into his mouth, but my gaze remains on Harlen as the leaves of the trees around us rustle from the light breeze. Harlen looks down at me, and as his eyes trace my body, there is a softness in his expression that makes my heart flutter. North's fingers trail over my skin, leaving goosebumps in their wake, and I shiver under his touch. I twist my fingers in the towel beneath me as my body tries to adjust to the attention of all these men—one watching me, one touching me, and one licking me until I'm pushed over the edge.

"Eli," I cry out as my body shudders and my legs clamp his head between them.

"Fuck," Harlen grits out, and I look up in time to see him step closer and shift his hips.

North has his mouth open and Harlen comes on his tongue. Fuck, if that isn't one of the hottest things I've ever seen.

Before I moved to Maple Hollow, the sex I had was predictable, nice even, but not the intense, mind-blowing experience I always thought sex should be. Since moving here, my eyes have been opened to a lot of things, and now I know I could never go back. I think it's time I make sure Charles understands I am no longer his, and I never will be again.

Chapter Thirteen

Lily

After our swim, North drives us back to my house and as we approach, I call dibs on the first shower, which I know is silly because it's my house. I rush through the shower, but when I get back downstairs, I find they have already packed up for the day.

"You look nice," North says, causing both Harlen and Eli to spin around.

"Do you have a hot date?" Harlen jokes.

"Actually, I'm going to dinner with Charles after I judge today's cook-off."

Harlen's face drops. "Oh."

I sigh. "I want to give him closure, and if I'm being honest, I need it as well. There was a time I loved him, and while he treated me poorly, I need to close that chapter of my life. Now I'm happy here and want to make a life for myself, but I have no idea what I will do when my money runs out. I also don't care either—I know I'll figure it out."

"That sounds fair," North says. "It's always good to have closure."

"Thank you," I say, not that I was asking for their permission. "I really want to explore what this is between us. We have so much to talk about, but it's only fair that I close off my last relationship completely before starting anything new."

Harlen's jaw clenches. "I hate knowing he ever touched you, and it pisses me off how I feel this way. On the outside, I'm this fun-loving guy, but inside, I'm so damn jealous and possessive."

Eli snorts. "That's an understatement."

"Charles is my past. He never made me feel what any of you have, even if I didn't know it was really you. But I don't know how this will work or even if it *can* be a long-term thing."

"Why don't you come over when you're done with Charles, and we can talk?"

"I would like that, but I don't know where you live."

Eli snorts. "We live on the top floor of the old hospital."

My mouth falls open—that explains so much. "You were not even meant to be part of the haunted house, were you?"

Guilt washes over Eli's face as he shakes his head. "I wasn't supposed to be on that night, but I saw you walking up the path and had to go downstairs to get a closer look. Harlen told me he met you when you came into town and how pretty you were. I wanted to see you for myself."

"Why did you chase me that night?"

He smirks. "Because you wanted me to."

North takes my hand. "How about I drive you to the town square, and then we will go home and wait for you?"

I agree and North leads me outside, while Harlen races to the truck and opens the passenger door, then helps me in. While he adjusts my seat belt, Harlen jokes about getting a room at the inn next to Charles's so he can rail me into the wall as payback for how he treated me. I remind him Charles pulling up today and seeing three hot men in my yard shirtless was all the payback I needed.

The town square is bustling with people. North drops me near the diner, and they all wave me off as I cross the street and find the judges' table.

"Lily, you made it," Mrs. Morgan says. "Here, take a seat beside Tom. The other judges are Mary Sue—the pastor's wife—and Leila, a teacher at the high school."

"Hi," I say with a small wave as I take the seat between Tom and Leila. Thankfully, Tom's grandmother holds his attention.

"I haven't introduced myself yet, and I've been meaning to say hello. It's not often we have new people move into town; I think I was one of the last." Leila leans in closer. "And between you and me, I'm not sure I fit in here all that much. I really need a normal friend."

I chuckle. "Girl, I feel that. Everyone seems too nice, if that's even possible."

"Right? I just want someone I can drink wine with on a Friday night, complain about the teenagers I teach, and have a good laugh."

Leila looks a few years older than me, but I think I might have just found a new friend. We swap social media information as Mrs. Morgan puts some plates down in front of us. The plates are numbered, so we don't know who has cooked what dish. Tonight there is a range of mains, sides, and desserts. We start with the sides, taking a small bite of each one and judging out of ten. Once those plates are cleared, we move to the mains, then the desserts. I may have to rethink dinner at this rate—I'm so full and don't think I could eat another bite.

Mrs. Morgan stacks containers into a bag and places them in front of me. "Here, take these and feed those men of yours," she whispers with a wink. I open my mouth to tell her they are not my men, but think better of it. It's no one's business what we are, and I'm sure they will appreciate the food.

Once we are done for the evening, Leila and I talk for a little while longer and organize to catch up next Friday for a girls' night. Then, with more pep in my step, I head toward the inn. While I still dread this conversation, I know it needs to happen. I can finally close this chapter of my life and move on.

When I walk into the reception area, a woman looks up from the computer. "Hi, welcome to the Firefly Inn. Do you have a reservation?"

"No, I'm here to see a friend, Charles Williamson. He's expecting me."

She smiles and nods. "Yes, he mentioned he'd have a guest tonight. He is room twelve. If you take the stairs, the doors are numbered."

"Thank you so much."

I leave her to get back to work and climb the stairs, finding his room easily enough and knocking on the door. Charles answers, and I take in the change of clothes. It's ridiculous how well put together he looks even when his button-down shirt is open at the front.

"Come in." He steps aside, holding his arm open. I walk past him, still clutching my bag of food for the guys, and take in the quaint little room. It's nothing flashy like he is used to, but I think it's cute and cozy.

"Do you want something to drink?" he asks, and I shake my head, deciding dinner with him definitely will not be happening.

"I won't be staying long. I have plans with friends tonight."

Charles rolls his eyes. "The same 'friends'"—he uses his fingers to make air quotes—"that were at your house earlier?"

I can't help my sigh. I knew this was going to happen. "Yes, Charles, those same friends. I came here as a courtesy to you, to offer us both closure. I loved you, and you broke my heart, but what we had is over. I have moved on and plan to make a life here."

"You really want to stay in this backward town? And

do what? Have you thought about that yet? What plans for the future do you have?"

I shrug my shoulders. "I don't know, but I will figure it out. Right now, I'm enjoying getting to know my family history, making new friends, and living my life."

"You need to come home. I have allowed this little tantrum, and now it's gotten out of hand. We have Thanksgiving plans with my parents and Christmas plans with your mother."

I scoff at him. "No, *you* have Thanksgiving plans with your parents, and *I* have Christmas plans with my mother. This is not a damn tantrum, Charles. I didn't expect you to want the same things I did, but you were not even willing to sit down and talk about it, to compromise and find things you *were* okay with. If you want to have vanilla sex the rest of your life, you can, but I don't want that. I want more, and—"

"So, you're fucking them, that's what this is about. Do they make you feel like a dirty whore, slap you around a little, and force themselves on you?"

Hysterical laughter peels out of me. "You know what? Fuck you, Charles. I'm not a whore just because I want to try new things. Sex should be fun and not a damn chore, which we booked in for every Wednesday night. I'm done with this conversation, and done with *you*. Leave town and never come back."

"We are not done, Lily," he seethes as I re-adjust my grip on the bag of leftovers, then storm toward the door. Turning back as I twist the handle, I smirk at him.

"We *are* done. If you cared about me, you would have had an adult conversation with me before you told your friends—you owed me that much. Yet now everyone knows my deepest fantasies, some I may never even be comfortable trying. You never loved me. I was a trophy for you to mold into the image you had for your life. One day you will find a girl who fits that image, and I wish you nothing but the best in life. You are a good man, and always treated me well, until you didn't. But I really hope you learn something from this and grow as a human being."

"Lily, please. I will do better," he begs as I open the door.

My eyes bulge when I see who is standing on the other side. "Eli," I whisper. "What are you doing here?"

"I was worried he would hurt you. I had to make sure."

Stepping into the hall, I pull the door shut and close my connection to Charles for good. Then I place my hand gently on Eli's chest. "Charles would never hurt me physically, though emotionally is another story."

"That's what I was worried about. But if he touched you, I would bury him."

"Come on, Brutus, let's go feed the others. I have leftovers from the cook-off."

Eli groans, and I let my hand fall away from his chest. I link it with his, and he looks down at our clasped hands as if it's an alien concept to him. Then his focus shifts to the aromatic bag in my other hand.

"Harlen's going to hump your leg if you bring him food."

I chuckle as we walk down the hall. "You know, I think I could be okay with that."

"Have I told you how perfect you are for us?"

"I do recall being told my pussy is perfect."

Eli snorts as we descend the stairs and then leave the inn behind. We head toward the town square again, because I need to stop and get some lady products from the grocery store, but he drops my hand as we get close. I reach for it again, and he stops abruptly.

"What's wrong?" I ask.

"You don't want them to think we're together, I'm the town leper, they—"

"I don't care what they think. I like you, Eli, and if I want to walk through town, holding your hand, I will. Unless you don't want people to think you're with me. Then I am okay with that."

His face contorts as if my words hurt him. "Lily, I would shout it from rooftops if we were together. You're new here and I don't want you involved in the rumors which will spread like wildfire. Everyone already has an opinion on us and our lifestyle, then adding you to that mix will be front-page news."

"Do I look okay?" I ask, and he nods, confused.

"You look beautiful, but you always do."

"Good, then I'm ready for my front-page photo. Let's give this town something to gossip about. But they don't all hate you, Eli. Mrs. Morgan specifically gave me this food to feed my male friends and winked at me. I think she secretly likes you all."

Eli laughs and takes my hand, lifting it to press a kiss

to my knuckles. We walk hand in hand through the town square. We even stop at the grocery store, where he takes the bag of food and still holds my hand while I pick up tampons. Honestly, I expected him to get weird about it, since Charles would always grab what he needed while I got my feminine products. The only time Eli lets go of my hand is to get chocolate from the shelf—he insists I should have all the things I need when I get my period. I try to tell him I can't eat my way through junk food, but he won't listen unless I give him a legit reason, one that doesn't have to do with gaining weight. He's already managed to crush my main argument. In the past, Charles had an image to uphold, so I watched what I ate, and while I didn't starve myself, I would always question if I needed that extra bite, and there were definitely no blocks of chocolate.

Eyes follow us through the store, and some people even stop and stare. Eli's size alone would be enough to make me stare. I know it makes him feel uncomfortable, and he is doing this for me, but screw this town. Eli has lived here most of his life, and whatever they think of his lifestyle, he should be able to walk through this town without being stared at like a damn zoo attraction.

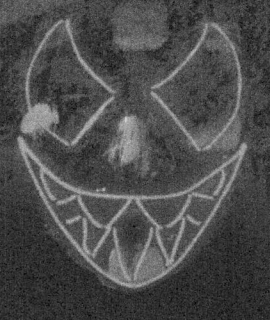

Chapter Fourteen

North

Lily and Eli stroll into the house hand in hand, and Harlen elbows me in the ribs as if I'm not already watching.

"I bring food," Lily chirps, and Eli holds up a plastic bag.

Harlen crosses the room in a flash, snatching the bag and inspecting its contents. "Oh, hell yes, cook-off food!"

We avoid the event because we refuse to support those who dislike us, but we won't turn down free food.

"Courtesy of Mrs. Morgan apparently," Eli muses.

"Is it poisoned?" Harlen asks skeptically. He takes the containers out of the bag and puts them down on the counter as I grab some plates and spread them out, along with the utensils. Harlen opens the lids and scoops out bits of everything onto his plate.

"Hey, ladies first," Eli growls.

"Shit! Sorry, I'm an animal," Harlen admits with a

laugh, and Lily smiles at him as if his caveman manners are funny.

"I couldn't eat any more if I tried. You three go ahead, and once you have served up, maybe we could talk."

"You're not breaking up with us already, are you?" Harlen asks, half joking.

Could he be any more stupid? Our situation is hard enough to navigate without him putting his foot in his mouth before we even get started. I whack him on the back of the head. "You can't end what hasn't started yet, idiot. Play it cool. I don't know about you, but I enjoy having her in our space."

Harlen laughs and carries his plate over to the table, not even bothering to heat it up. The guy eats cold food straight from the fridge most of the time. Eli and I serve ourselves, then heat the food up like normal people before taking our seats at the table.

"So what did you want to talk about?" Harlen asks, shoveling food into his mouth like it's his last meal.

Lily bites her lip and inhales.

I hate how her ex made her cautious to speak her mind when it comes to sex. "Don't be afraid to talk to us, Lily. We won't bite—"

"Unless you want us to," Harlen quips around a mouthful of food.

"Shut up," I snap at him. "We won't judge you or talk down to you. Even if we don't agree with what you say, we will always talk it through. That's why our situation works for us."

Eli places his hand over hers.

"I'm just worried about where we go from here. This is new, but I can see myself wanting more. I also know you have established relationships, and I will not come between you guys. It's still early days, but I suppose I want to know how it would all work. What if one of you decides you don't like me anymore? Will I lose you all?"

"They're all valid things to worry about. It is new, and I know I want to see where it leads as well. I don't think you need to be concerned about one of us not liking you, and as for our relationships, those would continue as they normally do. How yours forms with each of us as individuals or a group we would let develop organically."

She nods as I talk, then asks, "Do any of you get jealous?"

Harlen laughs. "I am guilty of getting jealous. As you know, I have a relationship with Eli and North. I'm very overprotective of Eli, but when North gets attention from the ladies, my jealousy always rears its ugly head."

Eli leans into Lily's side and whispers, "Just stick your finger in his ass—it fixes the problem straight away."

Harlen laughs and throws a carrot at Eli.

"In all seriousness," I interrupt, "if one of us is feeling a certain way, we call a family meeting and talk it through. Sometimes tempers can get the better of us, but we never make rash decisions or shame someone for feeling a certain way."

"That makes me feel better. Charles was not willing to listen to me and shamed me about what I might have wanted. I couldn't be in a relationship like that again."

"I was thinking about that," I continue. "Would you

consider writing a list of things you want to try? Then we could sort them into two groups, like 'yes that's a go' and then things you might want to explore in the future. I'm guessing since you enjoyed being chased by masked strangers, some things might need prior consent. While I don't think any of us have too many limits, we can at least let you know the ones on your list that we are comfortable doing."

Lily's eyes water and we all watch her cautiously; none of us has much experience with women crying.

"Don't cry, trouble. We just want to help you."

My words make her cry even more. "I'm sorry—I'm just a little hormonal."

"She is due for her period," Eli loudly whispers.

"Oh shit, do you need anything? I'm sure we have painkillers somewhere, or I am happy to take one for the team and make you feel better," Harlen says, wiggling his brows at her. "Period sex doesn't scare me."

I run my hand down my face. He really needs to think before he opens his mouth some days.

"That's good to know." Lily chuckles and wipes her eyes. "I will work on a list."

"Can we backtrack to the jealousy thing for a second?" Harlen asks. "I want to lay it on the table that if we are doing this and seeing where things go, I think we—no, *I* need you to understand you are free to do whatever with the people in this room, but no one else."

Jesus. His steely stare and gruff tone are enough to freak *me* out. "What Harlen means to say is, if you want out of this agreement at any time, you only need to say the word. But while we are being intimate, we'd like you to keep it to those in this room, and that goes for us as well."

Lily laughs and we all stare at her. "You really think I'd have the stamina to add more men to this equation? Or are you forgetting the passing out from exhaustion part? As it is, I don't know if I can keep up with all of you."

Worry creases her brow, and I wonder what she's thinking. I don't press her because we can figure this out as we go. It's not easy navigating this with the three of us, and now adding a woman, it could get even more difficult. I need intimacy, not just sex, and that is what I get from Harlen. Whereas Eli is very submissive, yet dominant with Lily. But right now, we want to be what Lily needs, so maybe we start with something she wants to try, and work on her future list.

"This list . . . do you have something on it you're curious about?" I ask her.

As she looks up at me, her face turns a light shade of pink. Oh, she has been thinking about something.

"Out with it!" Harlen exclaims. "I don't have any hard limits, so lay it on the table and chances are I will do it."

"Well, earlier, when Eli was sucking you off, I wondered if there was a way we could all do it together."

Harlen's smile overtakes his entire face, and even Eli smirks.

"You mean, me fucking Harlen while he is in your ass and you're riding Eli?" Her eyes snap to meet mine as I answer, and she nods shyly. Anger fills me at how nervous she is about allowing herself to want certain things, and how one asshole made her feel this insecure.

"Oh, fuck yes!" Harlen whoops, jumping from his seat and pulling Lily out of hers. "Do you know how long it's been since North put his sexy cock in my ass? Let's do this."

"Now?" she squeaks.

"Now's good for me," Eli says, finally joining the conversation.

"We are always ready to fuck. The question is, are you ready? If not, we can save it for another day," I reassure her.

"Now is good for me," she says, letting go of Harlen's hand and pulling her shirt over her head. "Just lead the way."

Eli picks Lily up and throws her over his shoulder. Lily giggles, then squeals when Harlen slaps her ass. Eli stalks down the hall, kicking open Harlen's bedroom door, and both Harlen and I follow him inside. If Lily wants to see us all in action, that is exactly what she will get.

Harlen doesn't waste any time; he grabs me by the back of my head and smashes his lips to mine. Heat courses through my body, knowing Lily is watching us. Normally we don't all fuck together—I prefer a more private and intimate setting—but right now, I can be persuaded.

Harlen is an amazing kisser, and my heart races as his lips move against mine. His tongue slides between my lips as he takes charge, and his body presses close to mine. He grabs the back of my shirt, pulling it up, and we only break apart to rip it over my head.

Peeking over at Lily, I find she is already naked on the bed and Eli is smothering her body with kisses as she watches us.

"Let's focus on Lily tonight," I say.

"Are you sure?" Harlen whispers. "I know you need that closeness."

"I'm sure. Let's give her a pleasure overload."

Harlen laughs as he removes his clothes—he is usually the first to get naked.

As I kick off my pants, Harlen takes my hand and leads me to the bed.

"Can I taste you?" I ask the stunning woman before me, and she nods.

Sitting at the end of the bed, I take a mental picture of her spread out, needy and waiting. The way her pink pussy is wet with her arousal, the way her body is flushed with need, and how her back lightly arches as Harlen takes one of her nipples in his mouth while Eli's large hand traces every inch of her body.

I lift her right leg and place a kiss on her ankle, slowly trailing my lips up the inside of her leg. I let myself breathe her in, and she shivers, her legs attempting to close. Pressing them back open, I flick her clit with my tongue, and she squirms beneath me as I flatten it and lick her. I savor her unique flavor—her sweetness is like nothing I have ever tasted before. She bucks her hips and I take them in my hands, putting my mouth right where she wants me. She grinds herself against my face, and I guide her body, letting her know she can fuck my face and breathing is optional for me at this moment.

"Fuck! Please don't stop! I feel like you're all everywhere."

At her mewls of pleasure, my tongue pushes inside her, and Harlen's finger works her clit.

"Bite me, Eli. I'm going to come!"

I don't know what Eli is doing, but she screams. Her ass lifts off the bed and her muscles clamp around my tongue. Harlen moves closer, twisting his fingers in my hair and lifting my head. Lily's eyes are focused on me as Harlen licks across my lips, cleaning her arousal from my face.

"Oh, fuck, that's hot," she blurts out as her chest heaves.

Slipping off the bed, I watch as Harlen lifts Lily gently from the mattress so Eli can situate himself. Eli's hand wraps around his thick, veiny cock, and he strokes himself a couple of times before Harlen helps Lily straddle his lap. Lily whimpers as she watches Harlen spit on Eli's length and use his own hand to spread his saliva around. Then he guides the fat head inside Lily's waiting pussy, and her head falls back on a moan as she slowly sinks down.

"Ride him for a few minutes, up and down, so North and I can see how well you take his massive cock. I want to see your juices coating him."

Lily lifts herself up as Eli grips her ass and spreads her cheeks apart, giving us the perfect view as she bobs up and down. While I watch the way Lily is stretched wide, and how her perfect pussy wraps around the fattest cock I've seen, Harlen retrieves the lube from his bedside table. He squirts a fair amount on his fingers and spreads it onto Lily's ass, then slips two fingers inside.

"Check out how good our girl looks with my fingers in her ass as she rides Eli's cock. Tell me how well you can take us."

Lily freezes, and I don't expect her to say anything. Harlen might be a talker in the bedroom, but not everyone is. "I'm taking Eli's cock so well, and your fingers are making me even wetter. Please fuck my ass, Harlen, I want to feel you."

"God damn, your wish is my command. North, get your fine self over here. You're going to fuck me so hard it sets the momentum for our fuck chain."

I smile at the idiot. One thing I like to do is film and rewatch. "Lily, can I record this on your phone? I want to rewatch your face later."

She nods. "It's in my shorts pocket." She moans as Harlen removes his fingers and circles her ass with the head of his cock, teasing her. Quickly I find her phone and set it up on the bedside table. We might not all be in frame, but I only want to see her face, to see her come while we are all fucking her. I find the right angle, and we are all in the shot minus Eli's face—no offense to him, but his isn't the face I want to see coming.

"I'm so full—shit, keep going," Lily moans.

"You're doing perfect. Look at how sexy you are. I can feel Eli's cock, and you both feel so good."

Moving closer, I wait for Harlen to be balls deep in Lily's ass before I find the discarded lube and squirt only a little on my finger. Harlen's a whore for pain and hates when I go easy on him. He would prefer I thrust inside him unprepared, but for Lily's sake, I want to take it easy. Having two dicks inside of you wouldn't be a walk in the park.

"Lily, I want you to circle your hips, grind your clit against Eli."

Eli and Harlen keep perfectly still as Lily circles her hips. She moans, and I'm so fucking hard hearing her sounds that I could use my precum as lube. Harlen looks at me over his shoulder and winks—he knows just what I need. Wetting my cock with the lube, and keeping most on the head, I press against his hole. This isn't our first rodeo, and I slide right inside, inching in slowly.

"Oh fuck, I think I found heaven," Harlen grits out, his head thrown back.

I roll my hips forward, pushing Harlen into Lily. Eli grunts, his fingers digging into Lily's ass. It's slightly awkward at first, but within a minute, we are all moving together in unison.

Harlen shouts his praise. "Fuck, Eli! Your cock feels so good, sliding against my cock. And our beautiful girl, she takes us so well. Oh, fuck . . . North, move your hips like that again. God, you all feel so good."

Harlen loves to dish out praise. It isn't something we ever had as children, and he has taken it upon himself over the years to shower us with compliments. It started if we did well at school, or if we made a meal he liked, and now every day he reminds us how well we are doing—and it's no different in the bedroom.

From this angle, I can't see much of Lily, but Eli holds her tight to his chest, and his fingers stroke her spine.

"I'm going to come," Lily shouts.

I thrust faster, changing up the speed a little, but not enough that she will lose her orgasm. I'm so close.

Lily cries out in pleasure, and Harlen pulls her up a little by her hair. "Fuck, you're perfect, Lily. Can you feel me coming in your ass, claiming you? I'm making you *mine*."

There is no jealousy when he says he's making her his. Harlen is possessive—he had nothing as a child and now he likes you to know when you're his, and he likes everyone else to know as well. Harlen's movements grow jerky as he comes, his ass squeezing me so tight I lose my resolve and finish with him. Eli moves Lily's hips for her, while we are all piled on top, and he also comes within seconds.

"Now *that* we will do again," Lily pants out, followed by a husky laugh as we fall on the bed, surrounding her in a sweaty heap.

She is right, we will be doing more of that, but next time I plan to be buried deep inside her little pussy. And once I catch my breath, we are watching it back, so I can see the pure bliss on her face. Then she can choose to delete it or keep it for her spank bank. I hope for my sake it's the latter because I will happily watch it over and over again with her.

Chapter Fifteen

Lily

Thanksgiving and Christmas came and went. My mom didn't make a scene about Charles and was surprisingly nice to the guys. Writing the list wasn't easy, but with their help, we managed to split it into things I was ready to try, and a few things I wasn't sure about but would proceed with caution.

My life is perfect, and I have found a natural rhythm and relationship with each of the guys individually. It was a combination of needing to get to know them on a personal level and wanting to know their personal likes and dislikes. I've discovered Eli loves to bury his cock inside me while we sleep, and North loves to kiss for hours, just exploring each other's bodies. Harlen seems to like everything, but he recently told me he wanted to have sex with me while I was asleep, and with my consent it became a mission for him to get the others to fuck me into a delirious mess and pass out. North then wanted to film it, and I have to say, watching his one successful attempt was hot as fuck.

For my comfort, all the videos are recorded on my phone and stored in a vault, which is password protected. I respect them so much for making me feel safe and secure. I really couldn't have asked for better men, and it still blows my mind I'm saying men, *plural*. The town didn't take it well at first. As predicted, Eli and I were front-page news after we walked through town hand in hand—the picture of him holding my tampons is cut out in our scrapbook—and the amount of times we have made the front page in the last few months is laughable.

Tonight, we are trying something else on my list. I want them in their masks, and I want them to be rough and hurt me. This has been a hard limit for North, as he wanted us to have trust before we got to this point—and a safe word. He has been honest; he doesn't know how big of a part he will play. He has drawn the line at any of them using a closed fist, and the others agreed. I'm excited and giddy. While it might seem odd, we have spoken about it at length. We've even written lists of what it would involve, with each man pointing out what they would be comfortable doing. Harlen is okay with slapping me, while Eli is okay with choking. Knowing all this doesn't make it any less exciting. I want to experience what it's like, and how much I will enjoy it. I won't know until it happens, but I'm so happy I get to experience it with them.

For North's sake, I went to the diner and got us dinner so we can have a nice meal beforehand and make him comfortable in his decision to at least try this tonight. Even if he leaves, if he can't watch, I trust all three of them with my body and my heart. I don't know if I would go as far as saying I love them yet, but right now we are all happy with how things are going.

The feeling of being watched has me on edge. It happened on the way to the store, and I thought it was Eli, but when he does it and he can see me growing worried, he makes himself known. People might think it's creepy how he follows me around, but he admits he does it, and I am okay with that. Our dynamic works on trust and communication.

Looking behind me again, I see no one there. Maybe my mind is playing tricks on me because I know what is going to happen after dinner.

"Someone help me, please. I'm stuck!"

I whip my head to the left toward the cemetery. "Leila?" I call out.

"Lily, please help me," she cries. "I fell over and can't get up."

"I'm coming," I call into the darkness. Our dinner drops to the ground, and I run as fast as I can toward the cemetery.

"I'm near the mausoleum. Please hurry!"

Cutting right, I run toward where she is. I know it well, as Eli and I come out here sometimes when he shows me all his favorite graves, though most died long before either of us was born. My heart races in my chest—I hope Leila isn't hurt. She's my only female friend here, unless you count Mrs. Morgan, who secretly pops over for coffee once a week. I think she's living vicariously through me, and she likes to watch the guys work, not that they really have much left to do anymore. North convinced me to renovate the bathroom and update things since there was mold on the ceiling. I agreed because his puppy-dog eyes got to me, and North in a tool belt and no shirt is a fantastic sight.

Slowing as I near the mausoleum, I search for where she could be. A twig snapping behind me has me whirling around, and a red glow mask illuminates the darkness. Oh shit, do they know Leila is hurt as well?

"Leila!" I call out, but she doesn't answer.

"She can't save you," Eli's husky voice calls out. I spin to look for his mask, and it lights up to my left.

"I need to help my friend."

Harlen steps out of the shadows. I know who they are now, even with the masks. He is holding something up in the air.

"Someone help me, please. I'm stuck!" I can see the audio track lighting up the phone Harlen is holding.

"You better run," North shouts.

"And don't get caught," Harlen calls out as I take off running.

These assholes had it all planned out. I push myself faster, knowing they will be hot on my heels, and I keep to the cemetery, heading toward their house. I chance a glance around for their masks, my adrenaline getting the better of me, and I trip over a fallen branch, landing face-first in the dirt beside an old grave. Their footsteps thunder right behind me.

"Please don't hurt me," I cry.

A hand wraps around my hair and pulls. I bring my hands up to grip his wrists, knowing deep down it's Eli. When he has me on my knees, he crouches over me.

"Be scared, little girl. We are going to own you."

I shiver at the sound of his voice, like I always do. One word out of his mouth makes me so damn wet I could become a slip and slide.

He drags me to my feet and then loosens his hold. Twisting my body, I kick out. The tip of my toe collides with his junk, and he groans, stepping back. I'm not sure where the others are or why they split up, but I run, giving it everything I have. His footsteps grow closer and I'm no match for him when he finally grabs me around the waist and slams my back against a large tree. It almost knocks the wind out of me, and one of his big hands wraps around my neck so tightly my body goes into fight-or-flight mode. I grab at his arms and dig my nails in deep, breaking his skin.

"You fucking whore, you're going to pay for that," he growls, letting go of me, and I drop to the ground, gasping for air.

I'm ready to fight. Shoving both my hands into the dirt, I gather a handful, and as he bends down, I flick the dirt from my hands at the holes in his mask. He grunts in surprise as he takes three steps back and turns his back to me. I scramble to my feet and spot the clearing for the house, but as I dart into the open, Harlen cuts across it. My eyes widen and I keep running. The door leading to the lower level is open, and if I push hard enough, I have a slight chance of beating him there. I reach the door, but this time I find no Halloween decorations inside—they have all been taken down. As I sprint through the room and reach the second door, I turn back and see him standing in the doorway, his chest rising and falling.

He steps forward, and I fling the second door open, then I run straight into North. A scream peels from my lips as I fall back onto my ass. I'm winded, so I use my moment on the floor to get my breath back, but North leans down and throws me over his shoulder.

"Put me down," I scream. It sounds louder now we are inside. I beat my fists against his back as he walks further into the lower level and through an open door. Looking around, I see they have set it up well. There's a dingy, old bed and a metal table with a rope rolled up on top. North throws me roughly onto the bed, causing my teeth to clack together.

Harlen picks up the rope, just as Eli steps through the door. He closes it and flicks the lock. Harlen moves closer, rope in hand, then he reaches out to grab me. My right hook throws him a little off balance, and his hand strikes out. His slap has my head falling to the side, and I tumble from the bed.

"Get up," he demands.

"Fuck you," I spit, scrambling backward.

The room is otherwise empty, with nothing I can use to defend myself. The three of them surround me and I can't fight them off. Eli moves in quickly, grabbing my arms and forcing them behind my back as I struggle against his hold. North steps in closer to me with Eli's switchblade and starts to slice my clothes straight from my body, while Harlen moves out of my sight, the rope in his hands. Once I'm naked, I feel him bind my arms behind my back.

"I'm going to have so much fun destroying you," Harlen rumbles near my ear, his voice deeper than normal and laden with dark intention.

"Stop, you're hurting me," I cry out as Harlen tightens the rope more.

Eli steps in front of me and squats down. I see a hint of his eyes behind the mask, and he winks at me. "Open up."

Instead, I clamp my mouth tighter, and he laughs as he takes my face in one hand and squeezes until my mouth opens. He then wedges something between my lips—it's a cross between a mouth guard and an O, and it forces my mouth to stay open. I can't talk and spit starts to pool in my mouth.

I'm pulled to my knees by the rope.

"Now the fun really begins," Harlen says, stepping around me and undoing his zipper. "I'm going to fuck your throat and there is not a thing you can do to stop me."

North moves to the corner of the room, while Eli holds my head. Harlen steps forward and pushes his hard cock through the O. He groans as he reaches the back of my throat, causing me to gag, and spit rolls down my chin. He fucks my mouth as if I were Eli, rolling his hips back and pushing in further with each thrust, making my eyes water and my jaw ache.

I try to push past the pain, then Eli roughly tugs me back, giving me a much-needed break as I gasp for air. Right when I think Harlen will slip back between my lips, Eli lifts me to my feet and drags me over to the metal table. He lays me sideways on it, flat on my stomach, with my legs hanging loose. He doesn't speak, but simply grabs my legs and zip-ties my ankles together, clearly not trusting I won't kick him in the nuts again. North pushes off the wall, and I follow him with my eyes until I can no longer see him. In fact, I can't see any of them. Someone steps up behind me, and runs a hand over my ass, then brings it down with a crack—once, twice, and the third time, it's right on my pussy, forcing a whimper from me as my drool collects below me on the cold metal. Eli comes back into view for a split second and pulls out what looks like a pillowcase from his back pocket. I struggle again, but my screams are muffled by the device in my mouth, which he pops out and then lifts my head, sliding it inside the black pillowcase. He doesn't tie it off, but it leaves me in complete darkness.

Suddenly, there's the scuff of boots as one of them steps up behind me, and he sheathes himself balls deep in one thrust, catching me off-guard. No one talks, which is causing my head to play tricks on me. We have a safe word, but I don't plan to use it. They know I crave the sound of Eli's voice, or Harlen's praise, or the way North strokes my hair or my arm if things are a little out of his comfort zone, but right now I'm alone, and hot tears spill from my eyes. I'm glad North can't see me like this.

Realization hits me—it's North inside me. His dick is

slightly curved and hits a spot which has me dripping without him even trying. He thrusts hard and presses down on my back. While he may not be using words, I can feel him telling me he's here and giving me what I need. When he pulls out after several more punishing strokes, I feel the loss of him, but he is quickly replaced with Eli, who stretches me out in a way uniquely him. He doesn't go hard; instead, he pulls back excruciatingly slow. Eli teases me, making my walls clamp around his shaft as they try to suck him back inside me, and he draws me nearer to an orgasm but stops before I reach the peak. When I whimper, he pulls out, and I'm lifted like a rag doll and laid face-down on the lumpy mattress, then someone climbs onto the bed and leans over me.

"Do you need to orgasm?" Harlen asks, pushing two fingers inside me and curling them to rub along my G-spot, making my body shudder.

"Yes, oh god, yes!"

"What a dirty girl, wanting a stranger to make her come," he whispers, his breath feathering against my skin, and I shiver. He removes his fingers and repositions himself, then his cock slides between my cheeks as he moves his length up and down, his precum smearing against my skin. I can only move enough to push my ass up and entice him to make the throbbing between my legs stop. I still can't see anything past the pillowcase, though I can sense Eli and North beside me, watching us.

"Do you want to know a secret?" he asks, but doesn't wait for my answer. "They like to watch you struggle, all tied up for us. And when I'm done, you will be covered in our cum, marked by us, and you will be stuck here forever. Do you want to be ours?"

"Yes, mark me, make me yours," I pant, and he does.

Harlen slides between my closed thighs, finding the wetness with ease, and he pushes inside me. He rolls his hips over and over, letting my orgasm build, then he leans down over me while supporting most of his weight, and my whole body thrums in anticipation. His lips tease the sensitive skin along my neck, then he sinks his teeth into my shoulder, and I'm gone, thrown over the edge, my pussy spasming around him as I scream a string of jumbled non-words. Harlen releases my shoulder and straightens, then warm wetness lands across my back while Harlen is still inside me. He curses as he thrusts in deep, then goes still, the swelling and pulsing of his cock the only movement.

"You're ours, Lily, and we are never letting you go," Eli says, removing the pillowcase from over my head.

North's eyes go wide when he notices the tears in mine, and he steps forward and caresses my damp cheek as Harlen pulls out of me and undoes the ropes. Once he is done, North scoops me into his arms, places a kiss on my head, and tells me he will take care of me. And that is exactly what he does. He takes me upstairs and places me in Harlen's bed, then climbs in behind me and pulls me into his body. Eli and Harlen are not far behind, and they spend hours holding me, touching me, and telling me how perfect I am.

"Do you really want me to be yours forever?" I ask them as the sun peeks through the curtains.

"Yes," they say in unison.

Sometimes when life gives you lemons, you just have to roll with it. Sometimes things work out perfectly because of the curve ball. I would never have expected Charles to do what he did, but if he hadn't, I wouldn't have moved to Maple Hollow to live in my deceased grandmother's house. And I definitely wouldn't have met these three amazing men, who are determined to let me experience what I like without shame or feeling different. And who knows? Maybe one day the people of Maple Hollow will be okay with them chasing me through the town square. I snort at the thought. Yeah, some things won't ever happen, but that's okay because my masked men will chase me anyway.

The End

ALSO BY JAYE PRATT

G.O.D.S Series.

G.O.D.S

Checkmate

Endgame

G.O.D.S Next Generation

Zhavia

Zadom

D'Arco Mafia Duet (Italian Mafia)

Liar Liar Part One

Liar Liar Part Two

O'Brien Mafia Duet (Irish Mafia)

Beautiful Liar Part One

Beautiful Liar Part Two

Knox Academy
(Complete Series)

F*ck You

F*ck Off

F*ck Yeah

F*ck Her

Grand Ridge University

Tens - The Invitation

Tens - The Takeover

Tens - The Revelation

With you I am home

(Complete Duet)

Boys like you

Girl Like me

Duet (recommended to read this version it has a bonus scene.)

Standalones

Sweetest Venom (DARK WHY CHOOSE ROMANCE)

Chad and his not harem (WHY CHOOSE ROM COM)

Brad and the girl off limits (MF AGE GAP)

Vada and the boy next door (YA ROMANCE)

Street Rat (WHY CHOOSE MAFIA)

Diesel (MF ACADEMY ROMANCE)

Hate us like you mean it (WHY CHOOSE ROMANCE)

Love me like you mean it (MM ROMANCE)

Silence (ROCKSTAR ROMANCE)

STALKER LINKS

Bookbub

Newsletter

Facebook

TikTok

Reader Group

Instagram

(All of my paperbacks are for sale on my Merch store. These all come with my signature. Postage worldwide.)

For spoilers and Trigger warnings for all of my series visit my website.

Website

ABOUT THE AUTHOR

Jaye Pratt

Jaye is an Australian author who lives in Queensland. Her love of reading came later in life after her sister forced her to read the twilight saga and she hasn't looked back since. Reading has become an escape from reality, a way to relax and forget about life for a short while.

Jaye is a mother of six children and two grandchildren, and she loves having a large family. If Jaye isn't writing, you will find her being a referee to a handful of her children or being a mum taxi, dropping children at work or sport.

ACKNOWLEDGMENTS

Tee - For being my rock, my sounding board and keeping me on task even if I do get mean.

My Ferals - I stand by the fact that without you all I would be super rich, but lucky for me you are all here and now I have to work to support you because you all think you have money.

Samantha bloody Barrett - Why do I even like you again? You don't read my books, you are super mean and I'm not sure I should associate with a swamp troll like you. Oh I remember its because my bestie is related to you and I have to keep you around for her.

Cat Jay PA & Kelly Messenger, you are an editing super team. Thank you so much for the work you put into this book. Kelly you know how to super charge a sexy scene .

The street team girls, I don't know why you all stick around when Samantha's books keep releasing and you have to feel obligated to pimp them out. So thank you for your hard work, you know her books are a hard sell and she needs all the help she can get and thank you for reading and loving Don't get caught.

My Beta girlies and Arc readers, thank you

for reading and supporting me with all of my books, you will never know how much this means to me.

Lastly my **Readers** who no matter what, will pick up anything I write and support my dream. You all bloody rock.

Made in United States
Orlando, FL
24 June 2025